The Big

That very night was the night. The
future.

Liz's dad works on the North Sea
and two weeks at home. The job is
rigs are past their best, but when George comes home he spends all his time in the pub, getting drunk and aggressive and terrorizing his family. They are all relieved when he goes back to the rig.

Liz's only escape from her home life is her music. She has played the saxophone since she was old enough and now she is part of a band – The Rhythm Sisters. They are due to play in a gig at the Town and Country Club, which could be the big break Liz is hoping for — but then comes news that could ruin everything . . .

Louise Hide was born in Chichester, Sussex and started writing at the age of eight. She did not do well at school and describes herself as self-educated through her love of reading.

She has had a very diverse career, working in hotel management, as an au-pair, a psychiatric nurse, an estate agent, and an advertising copy-writer. She has worked in Germany and France and is now a playwright and novelist working from her home in London. Her latest play was performed at the Edinburgh Festival in 1995 and she has had two novels published. *The Big Break* is her first book for Oxford University Press.

Cover design and illustration by Slatter-Anderson

The Big Break

Louise Hide

Oxford University Press
Oxford New York Toronto

Oxford University Press, Walton Street, Oxford OX2 6DP

Oxford New York
Athens Auckland Bangkok Bombay
Calcutta Cape Town Dar es Salaam Delhi
Florence Hong Kong Istanbul Karachi
Kuala Lumpur Madras Madrid Melbourne
Mexico City Nairobi Paris Singapore
Taipei Tokyo Toronto

and associated companies in
Berlin Ibadan

Oxford is a trade mark of Oxford University Press

First published 1996

A CIP catalogue record for this book is available
from the British Library

ISBN 0 19 271678 6

Printed and bound in Great Britain by
Biddles Ltd, Guildford and King's Lynn

For my dear friend Michael Tobin.
And in memory of Emilio Varvelo.

1

In 1968, oil was discovered in the North Sea.

During the seventies, a tapestry of oil fields was opened; it stretched almost from the Scottish mainland to the Arctic Circle, and fanned out across hundreds of miles of water off the coasts of East Anglia and the East Midlands. Massive installations weighing hundreds of thousands of tons were dragged out to sea by tugs and lowered on to piles driven almost 400 feet into the sea bed. The drills then went to work, turning oil and gas reservoirs which had lain undisturbed for aeons into leaky sieves. Before long, millions of barrels of oil and cubic feet of gas began to be dispatched back to shore through a spaghetti junction of pipelines.

The discovery of oil in the North Sea heralded the dawn of a brand new era of hope. Hope for the country. Hope for the oil companies. And hope for the armies of engineers, scientists, labourers, caterers, administrators and the thousands of companies that would supply the industry with everything from protective gloves, to soap and paint stripper.

Oil had produced a well of opportunity for everyone. Men flocked from all over the country to work on the rigs; they came from shipyards, from building sites, from motorways, and the merchant navy. And they came from local fishing communities; small towns and villages dotting the coastline and which had trawled a living from the sea for generations. When the local fishermen threw in their nets and took up their hard hats, these tiny enclaves were rocked to the core as the oil industry gnawed into centuries of tradition and heritage by the minute.

But everyone knew those great iron monsters couldn't fight off the elements of the North Sea for long. Within twenty years, the rigs were beginning to pass their 'sell-by' date. They were breaking up, patched together by a series of welds; welds on welds on welds. They were unstable. Unsafe. Everyone knew. Many pretended not to.

George Dean had grown up in the small fishing community of Boughton on the Norfolk coast. Instead of following his father on to the trawlers, he had trained as a welder and got a job on the rigs, spending two weeks on and two weeks off shore every month.

Every time George was home, he made a couple of trips to Norwich and always found himself being propelled towards the second-hand record shop. When he got home, he usually had at least two battered old LPs tucked under his arm that he had salvaged from the 'two-for-the-price-of-one' bin. He would poke his head around the living room door and grunt, 'Play your cards right and I might have something for you.'

Liz leapt off the chair. 'Let's have a look, Dad. Let's have a look.'

'I said, I might.' George held the records behind his back and grinned slyly.

'Charlie Parker!' squealed Liz after she had wrestled the tatty sleeves from his grip. 'Put him on. Put him on, Dad.'

The green plastic gramophone did its best, whirling and wheezing out the great masters. George and Liz didn't care; they would sit on the old brown sofa for hours, listening, snapping a finger, tapping a foot, shrugging a shoulder, or two, like laughing hyenas.

In the middle of it all, George threw his head back and said, 'The night I saw Charlie Parker was the night I knew God made Heaven and Earth.'

'I thought that was the night you saw Louis Armstrong.'

'The night I saw Louis Armstrong I knew Paradise was just around the corner.'

Later George would take his trumpet out of its case and rub it on his sleeve. 'Let's have a blast then,' he said, starting to play to the record. Then he'd count Liz in, she'd pick up her clarinet and begin to play too.

How they played. On and on. On and on and on and on. Not noticing the time. Over and over the same piece, time and time again. George's patience was infinite when it came to jazz. 'Look. Like this,' he said. 'Come in here, on "E". Listen to me a minute.'

Soon they were playing the track, and then the whole record.

When Liz was ten, George smuggled her out of the house one night and bundled her into the back seat of the Vauxhall. Soon they were driving around the back streets of Norwich. It was pouring with rain and everything was shining and shimmering and gleaming under the street lights. It was like Las Vegas.

George stopped the car outside a door which had a neon sign above it saying The Pied Piper. 'Stay there,' he said, and went to talk to the man on the door.

Five minutes later, Liz found herself creeping around the back of the building. She and George were drenched and stood like drowned rats in the alleyway, waiting for the man to open the Exit door. 'Make sure you sit round the side where no one can see her,' he growled when he finally appeared. He had smarmed his hair down with grease and looked as though he had been standing in the rain all night, even though he hadn't ventured a toe outside once.

On stage a jazz band was playing; keyboard, double bass, drums, trumpet, and sax. George and Liz sat down at a small table tucked away from the rest of the crowd. As soon as George saw the band he came alive. He couldn't take his eyes off the stage for a moment. He even forgot to order drinks. 'Look at that,' he said to Liz, wide-eyed and grinning. 'That's Bobby up there on the double bass and Yonkers on the keyboard. Get an earful of them, then.'

And Liz was getting an earful. She couldn't believe she was there. Every part of her body tingled as she stared through the thick, smoky atmosphere, entranced by all those people, all those grown-ups. She sat on the edge of her seat pretending to be grown up too. She *was* grown up. No one looked at her. No one thought it strange that she was there, and only 10 years old.

'Before you . . . ' George hissed, ' . . . is what's left of The Rumbabas. I was part of that once.' He looked at Liz for a second and smirked. 'Yeah, me, your old dad.'

Liz turned and looked at George. She was bubbling with pride. Her dad, a Rumbaba. Up there, on the stage, with all those people looking. It was hard to believe.

'I want to see you up there one day,' George hissed into her ear. And then he hailed the waiter and ordered a drink.

On the way home Liz was very quiet. She felt tired but her mind was racing, still tingling with the excitement of it all. The band had played all her favourite tunes: 'Take Five', 'Summertime', 'Misty', 'Take the A Train'. She knew them all. Could play most of them.

The Rumbabas had mesmerized Liz from the moment she set eyes on them. She studied their movements, watched how they played, made mental jottings of their techniques. She even sat riveted when they took a break and hurled pints of watery beer down their throats.

As they purred home in the car, she suddenly announced to George, 'When I'm old enough, Dad, I want to play the sax.'

One afternoon, George walked through the back garden carrying a huge cardboard box. 'Blimey, Dad, what on earth have you got there?' Liz called out from the top of the conker tree. She shinned down it in two seconds flat and charged into the house.

But George wasn't letting on. He winked at her and then tore into the box with the big scissors Sheila used for cutting up bacon.

'A new record player! Bloody hell! Where did you get it?'

'Newsons. It's brand new. So don't bloody break it.' George looked at his daughter and screwed up his bushy eyebrows.

But Liz was too excited to take any notice. 'Let's put it on. Put it on. Come on, Dad. Let me choose the record.'

Half an hour later, the new machine was still sitting there in all its glory. Pristine. Untouched. Wired up and plugged in. But with not a sound coming out of it. George and Liz stood looking at it gloomily. 'We must be doing something wrong,' said Liz despondently.

'That's obvious.'

George picked up the arm again and dropped it on to the record; it slithered across the vinyl and crashed on to the label. He looked at it for a moment longer, then shouted, 'Doesn't even bloody work.' He picked up the machine and plonked it back in its box. 'Right,' he said. 'It's going straight back to Newsons. Right now.' Then he picked up the box and stormed off.

Liz had been digging a swimming pool at the bottom of the garden. Progress was slow due to rain and landslide. She spent the whole afternoon picking away at it, looking up every few seconds to see if George had come back with the new record player. He had promised. He said he'd be back with it in full working order. But he never appeared.

He got 'stuck' in the pub.

The next day George had the whole thing up and running before Liz got home from school. At some point he sheepishly announced that he had forgotten to put a needle in. 'Bloody stupid that they didn't put one on in the first place,' he drawled. And before long the two of them were having 'a blast' to the 'new' music.

That was when Liz still had her clarinet.

'What the bloody hell do you think you're up to?' Sheila, Liz's mother, screamed when she saw the record player. 'You owe Arthur Lowe for all that work he did on the car and the twins have got to have new school uniforms.'

'All that's going to be taken care of,' George replied calmly, putting his hands out to quieten his wife down.

'How?'

'I've got a plan.'

'You've always got a plan. But nothing ever comes of them.'

'This one's different. I've been talking to Roger Drain and he's looking to expand his taxi fleet.'

'Expand his fleet! He's only got one car.'

'He'll have two now. When I'm home I'll do a bit of mini-cabbing.'

'And what am I supposed to do while you're swanning around in the car all day?'

'It's good money. We'll be straightened out in no time.'

'That'll be the day.'

George never did any taxi work. Sometimes he said he did, but he lied. He was down the pub instead. At one point Sheila thought he might be having an affair with Avis Chilton who worked in the Post Office and she sent Liz off to hang around Avis's house and spy on her. But George was never there, the car was always parked outside the Crown and Anchor. 'He couldn't have an affair with next door's budgie,' Sheila scoffed, her head buried in a car manual. She had decided to learn how to repair the car herself, seeing as no garage would give them the time of day any more.

When Liz was still young and George was away, she sometimes slept in her parents' bed with Sheila. She loved snuggling up to her mother's warm body. One night, when Liz was fast asleep in her own bed, she suddenly found herself being woken by Sheila. 'Come on, Liz. You're coming into our bed,' she said. Sleepily, Liz fell out of bed and stumbled across the corridor into her parents' room. It wasn't until she was tucked up in their bed that she suddenly remembered George was home.

'What about Dad?' she asked sleepily.

'I told him, if he's not back by eleven, he's not coming back at all,' Sheila snapped as she clambered into her nightie. 'I warned him. The house is locked.'

A shudder of fear passed through Liz. That day her parents had had the most almighty row because George had poured half his pay packet down his throat at the Crown and Anchor, and Sheila didn't have enough money to pay the rent. After the row, neither parent would speak to the other and so they passed messages via Liz:

'Tell your father he's full of crap.'

'Tell your mother "bollocks".'

That night, Liz lay in her parents' bed, petrified, waiting for George to come home. She could hear the big clock ticking in the hallway downstairs, the ugly one with a white plastic case that George's sister had given them. An owl hooted outside as it fluttered from tree to tree, surveying the cornfield for mice or moles, any unsuspecting creature willing to offer itself up as supper. She heard her older brother, Gary, stagger to the loo, half asleep. Sheila was pretending to be asleep too, but she wasn't. Her breathing was irregular and she tossed and turned in bed, moving around from one side to another. She knew that at any moment the silence would be broken and George would arrive back, drunk, and discover he had been locked out.

It happened just after two o'clock in the morning. He woke the whole household shouting below the bedroom window. 'Don't think you're locking me out of my own bloody house, you cow!'

Liz and Sheila lay in bed, frozen, petrified, like two rods. 'Just ignore the bastard,' said Sheila. She picked up a cigarette, lit it and tried to hide her trembling hand from Liz. But Liz knew she was afraid. She could see the glowing tip of the cigarette shaking in the dark. She could hear her heart pounding, noisily. Feel her fear rushing around the room.

Suddenly they heard a huge crash downstairs. George had smashed a window and was trying to haul himself into the house. Following much thudding, belching, and cursing, he finally staggered up the stairs, along the upstairs landing and flung open the bedroom door. He turned on the light and stood in the doorway, sneering down at Sheila and Liz who were huddled up in bed, pretending not to be afraid. He looked terrible; his hair was everywhere, his clothes covered in mud, and blood was dripping down the side of his face where he'd cut himself on the broken window. 'Don't ever make me break into my own house again,' he snarled.

'Get out of here,' Sheila snapped, pulling the bedclothes over her for protection.

'I bloody shan't. Not in my own house.' George stepped forward, glaring at Sheila. 'If anyone gets thrown out of this house, it'll be you.' He pulled the bedclothes back and grabbed Sheila by the arm, roughly trying to haul her out of bed.

Liz was terrified but still leapt to her mother's defence. 'Get off her, Dad,' she shouted standing on the bed in her pyjamas. She grabbed one of her father's hairy arms and bit deep into it. It seemed the right thing to do. Her mother was such a thin, defenceless creature. She needed protection.

'You little brat,' George shouted and, without thinking, he let go of Sheila and swiped Liz fast and hard around the face.

Two days later Liz still had a black eye. And a saxophone.

The day after Liz turned seventeen, she passed her driving test. All those hours kangerooing up and down the aerodrome with Sheila in the Vauxhall had finally paid off.

Now, Freedom!

That summer was a hard one. The sun had come out in May and refused to go away, even in September. They'd never known anything like it. 'The hottest since records began,' they said. Or, 'The worst drought since 1923. Lock up your hosepipes.' Everything was brittle and parched; the last gasps of life had been squeezed out of the banks and hedgerows which lay deadly still, unable to move, waiting for the sun to hibernate for the winter.

No one was used to heat like that. Not in Boughton. Not with it being so close to the North Sea. There was always a bit of a wind, a breeze, a hint. But not this summer. The air had remained trapped in an invisible cloud which lay suspended in the sky like a fat person which would never budge. Ever.

In her bedroom, Liz wiped the perspiration from her face as she stood in front of the mirror carefully combing her short dark hair backwards. Then she let her head drop forward and a thick clump of fringe flopped over one eye. She tucked a white T-shirt into a pair of baggy jeans shorts and then slung a black biker jacket over her shoulder. That was it. The look. Her look. None of the other girls in the town dressed like that. They all wore skimpy boob-tube things and leggings and mini-skirts. Liz couldn't. It just wasn't her. She had tried but she felt ridiculous. Sometimes the girls gave her a funny look and she felt awkward and self-conscious. Unfeminine. Clumsy. But she couldn't truss herself up like a Christmas chicken. She felt stupid.

Just as she was inspecting a blackhead on her chin, there was a rap on her bedroom window. She spun around in surprise. Sheila was peering in; she had two nails in her mouth and a hammer in her hand. 'Hold these for us,' her mother mumbled.

Liz opened the window and craned her head out of it to take a look at the guttering. 'It won't hold if you just bang a nail in,' she said.

'I know that. It's temporary in case we get another deluge. I thought we might go down the builders' yard tomorrow and get some more guttering.'

'I can't. I've got a practice session.'

'Then I'll have to get Dad to take me when he's home.'

Liz sighed. 'Maybe we can fit it in tomorrow morning. And, Mum, that ladder looks bloody dangerous. I'd better come down and hold it.' Liz tutted; her mother was always hanging upside down or wobbling around precariously on something. Once she'd mastered the mechanics of the car, she had taken an evening course in woodwork and now there was no stopping her. Any spare corner had been filled with shelves, chairs which had been unsafe for years were miraculously restored to their former rigidity and Sheila had even knocked up a bed for one of the twins.

Once Sheila had fixed the guttering, Liz went back to her room and practised on the sax for half an hour or so. Then she gave up. She felt tired and couldn't concentrate. She'd been woken at the crack of dawn by the twins, Bobby and Sue, whose Saturday morning ritual comprised cleaning out the rabbit hutch. Every week, without fail, Hettie managed to escape and the twins rushed around after her, squealing and shouting, and trying to scoop her up before she disappeared under the hedge and into next door's garden.

Liz laid the sax carefully in its case. Downstairs, the house was deadly quiet. Unusually so. Everyone had disappeared: Sheila, Gary, the twins. Everyone. And, of course, the house was spotless. It always was when George was coming home. Sheila had been up since seven that morning, cleaning and polishing like a woman possessed. She had probably taken the twins out somewhere so they wouldn't mess everything up again.

Liz didn't want to be around, waiting for George to arrive. Even though the house appeared orderly, the atmosphere was frenzied. It was as though someone had picked it up and given it a good shake. Sheila was like a nervous wreck, looking up at the clock every five seconds. And the twins got silly and tearful and excited and fearful, all in one go. He was meant to arrive at two o'clock that afternoon, but he wouldn't. He had been working off-shore for twelve years and had never once got back at the appointed time. Yet still Sheila waited. And waited. And waited. And then, when her husband did walk in through the door, she ignored him.

That's how it was in the Dean household.

When Liz went outside, the car was gone. As she had suspected, Sheila had carted the twins off for some fish and chips to keep them out of the house. So Liz leapt on her bike and started to peddle along Harborough Road towards the town. Suddenly, she saw her mother lurching towards her in the Vauxhall; the twins were in the back, rummaging through a cereal packet for the free giveaway. The car ground to a halt, making a terrible noise.

'The brake pads need changing,' said Sheila winding down the window and peering out. She had a cigarette between her fingers and a thin spiral of smoke unfurled from its tip and slipped out through the window into the stagnant heat of the day. 'Where are you off to, then?'

'Nowhere.'

'Well, make sure you see your dad before you go out tonight.'

'He won't be back by then.'

'He's *meant* to be back at two.'

'Mum . . . ?'

'I'm not saying anything.' Sheila took a long drag on the cigarette and stared ahead of her, her lips pursed.

'Can I take the car? If I can take the car, I'll get home earlier.'

'No,' said Sheila. 'I might need it.'

And that was the end of that because they both knew why Sheila might need the car, but neither wanted to say.

Boughton had always been a tiny hubbub of activity. Sitting on the edge of the North Sea on the way to nowhere, this small fishing community had kept itself pretty much to itself. The locals thought they were an enterprising lot, but they didn't have much to compare themselves with; half the population had never been further than Norwich, and only a handful as far as London. However, over the years, the village had ventured a few tentacles out into the surrounding countryside and these had taken root, expanding the community into a small market town. As they had predicted, 'new life' soon began to take over, the younger generation no longer wanted to be fodder for the insatiable North Sea and grabbed any opportunity which could save them from such a fate.

'New life', as they called it, arrived compliments of oil and gas conglomerates. In just twenty years Boughton had become the centre of the North Sea Southern Sector gas and oil industry; both commodities were pumped back from the rigs to a massive refinery in Boughton via huge pipelines which snaked along the sea bed. No more could you look into the sky without seeing helicopters clattering in and out to and from the shore like swarms of insects. Trawlers which were once stuffed with slimy, writhing fish had been transformed into supply or stand-by vessels and spent their whole time chugging off to the gas fields, or just hanging around the rigs, waiting for a disaster to happen.

And the people in the town were changing. Outsiders were moving in, large posh houses were being built in tree-lined avenues and delicatessens and restaurants were springing up in the High Street. Boughton was going through its own refinery process.

Liz glided into Cross Street on her bike. She passed the alms houses where they had found Joseph Craddock hanging in the nude only six months ago, and then she slowed down opposite the taxi office and looked in. No one was there. Only her older brother, Gary, and a couple of young kids. She knew Gary would be there, leaning against the counter, watching a couple of brats playing on the slot machines. He was a long, stringy thing. Skinny and nervous, like Sheila. He had a long face and thin blond hair which he always parted in the middle, making him look like a butler.

He worked at the Regal Bingo Hall on Saturday and Wednesday nights as a doorman, giving the pensioners the once-over as they hobbled in. It was a miracle he had held down this job for the whole summer season; it was the uniform that did it, he thought he looked dead smart in his droopy bow tie and moth-eaten black trousers with velvet stripes stumbling down them. George told him he looked ridiculous. Like a namby-pamby. But then George would.

Roger Drain's shiny head could just be spotted on the other side of the taxi office counter. These days, he had been relegated to the 'control room' and was bent over a battered radio bellowing out instructions to his wife, Muriel, who was cruising around town in *his* brown Cortina. He bellowed because it was *his* car, which *he* used to drive and which *he* had lovingly looked after for years. But then, one day, he was caught swerving down the High Street at over four times the limit and that was the end of that. Ceremoniously, he handed the keys over to his gloating wife, but secretly he could never forgive her for depriving him of his one pride and joy.

Karen had been sitting in the Sea Shell for at least an hour. She had managed to make one cup of tea last for most of it and was just thinking about ordering another when Liz walked in and threw herself on the torn plastic bench opposite her.

'Have you seen Mutley?' Karen asked immediately.

'No. Why?'

'Thought he might want to go into Norwich this afternoon.'

'Thought you might, more like,' said Liz picking up the menu and looking down it.

'You'll get salmonella eating in here.'

Liz threw the menu back on to the table, pulled her feet up on to the bench, leaned back against the wall and let out a deep sigh.

Karen watched her. She had always watched her. All their lives. They had grown up together, been to the same schools, played on the same beach, in each other's backyards. Now Karen could see her friend slipping away. Already, since they had both left school that summer, they were seeing less of each other. Liz was working part-time at the local hotel and Karen had been given a full time job at the fish and chip shop; of course, it wasn't what she would have chosen, her face had exploded into a carpet of greasy pimples and the heat was unbearable. But she needed the money, so it would have to do for the time being.

'Want to come into Norwich this afternoon?' she asked, rummaging through her handbag for a mirror.

Liz shook her head and ran her fingers through her hair. 'Dad's coming home today and Mum wants me around.'

'What, to help drag him out of the Crown and Anchor?'

'Probably.' Liz shrugged her shoulders. Everyone knew George's habits. Everyone knew he'd stop in the pub, just for a pint, just to say hello, and wouldn't emerge until he got thrown out. Everyone knew that. That was why Liz hated Boughton.

'Snot was asking about you at the King's Head last night,' said Karen. She found the mirror and started smearing lipstick over her thin, pallid lips. 'Aren't you interested?'

'Not really.'

'I think he's quite nice.'

'You go out with him, then.'

'He's never asked me, has he.'

That was Karen. Our Karen who drifted from one day to the next. Whose life revolved around mail-order catalogues and 'pulling power'. Her only goal in life was to get her own place—council was fine, even if she had to get pregnant for it.

'If you ask me, a career is a load of old squit,' she said in her low Norfolk drawl. 'I don't know what everyone's going on about. Find a half-decent bloke and he'll do all the work for you.' She crumpled her lips together, got up and teetered over to the counter, balancing precariously on a pair of white stilettos. Karen was always dressed to the nines, even in the chip shop when she was trussed up in an overall and hat. After all, you never know who you might meet.

'Can't get you a tea,' she said on her return. 'Haven't got any money left.'

Liz shrugged her shoulders. She hated the tea in the Sea Shell, it was always stewed and had greasy globules floating around on top of it. 'What's the point of going to Norwich, then?'

'Can look, can't I?'

Suddenly Karen spied Mutley walking past the café. 'Shit,' she muttered, clambering out from the seat and scooping up her handbag. 'And I've just bought that bloody tea.' She hobbled over to the door as fast as her stilettos would take her. 'Sure you don't want to come,' she yelled back to Liz as she clattered out.

'Not in that stinky car. It smells of armpit. Or worse.'

'You can have the tea. Pay me back another day.'

'Thanks a million.'

* * *

Liz didn't stay at the Sea Shell for long. She left the tea, jumped on her bike and started to peddle along the coast road towards the sea. When she got to the caravan site she braked sharply, sending the back wheel of the bike skidding out behind her across the sand.

Boughton had seen another scourge loom up over the years. A curse to some, a blessing to others. Whichever, it had invaded the town like a virus.

Caravans.

They came. They saw. They conquered.

Every year, from May to September, caravans of caravans plunged through the streets of Boughton. Swinging their hips like big girls, they tore at the hedgerows and stamped on verges with gay abandon. Regular meetings were held in the village hall where pros and cons would be fired like missiles across ripped canvas chairs. These meetings were always heated affairs; on the one side sat the profiteers (the publicans, the shop owners, members of the council, and Roy Hardcastle who owned the caravan site); and on the other side sat the losers (everyone else, and Millicent Brown who was guardian of the public lavatories—both Ladies and Gents—and had her work increased threefold during the summer without receiving any extra pay).

Liz shaded her eyes from the sun and looked across the site. There they all were, sitting there like giant maggots enjoying the view. There were battered, long, thin ones that belonged to Roy Hardcastle and sat on concrete feet all the year round; there were streamlined de luxe models which were lovingly deposited in the sand by their owners; and there were funny bubbly things which popped out of plastic sheeting or garages once a year.

And then there was the sea. The sea, the sea. In all its wonderful brininess. Slipping in, slithering out. Benign, innocuous. Insatiable, dangerous. Liz had known it to swallow people whole; one minute they were showing off in the waves, the next they were gone. Men, women, and children were sucked down like spaghetti. Older people swam out too far and ran out of steam, or had heart attacks, or cramp. No one heard their cries which were swept away by the wind and dispersed like pollen in tiny, fragmented whimpers.

'Oi, Liz!'

Liz swept around. Snot was standing behind her, squinting as he looked directly into the sun. She'd forgotten what a prat he was. He was one of those people who never went brown, he just went pinker and pinker and then all his skin began to peel away, leaving large exposed white patches of skin that looked like some nasty disease.

'Thought it was you,' he said.

'Hi,' said Liz coldly. She twisted her mouth, annoyed, and started to walk towards the sea. He followed her.

'I called you last night. Didn't your mum tell you?'

'Can't remember.'

'*The Exterminator*'s on up at the Regal. Thought you might want to go.'

'No thanks.' Liz stopped and looked at him for a minute. Don't be cruel, she thought. Be nice. 'It's just not my sort of thing, Snot,' she started to explain.

Encouraged by the softer than usual tone of her voice, Snot persevered. '*Love Song for Two* is on next week.'

'Forget it.'

2

'Drop us off at the Crown and Anchor, will you?' George said to the taxi driver on the way back from the heliport. 'I'll just pop in for a quick one with the lads.'

Famous last words. As usual, one drink led to another and George was firmly ensconced at the bar in no time. He never meant to stay all afternoon. He had every intention of drinking just the one pint. But something always happened. It was as though a secret force took hold of him and as soon as he finished his first pint he just couldn't say no.

'Want another one, George?'

'Oh, why not!'

'One for the road, George?'

'Go on then. But she'll have my guts for garters.'

Word soon got around that George was home and in the pub. Men from the town casually wandered in and hovered around the bar; they knew George was always good for a couple of pints because he always finished first and couldn't wait for everyone else to catch up. Mean he was not; he couldn't stand buying a drink for himself without offering everyone else one too.

Men drifted in and out of the Crown and Anchor all afternoon. By around five, the pub was virtually deserted and George sat perched on the stool, feeling extremely drunk. Bill, the publican, had disappeared into the back room and was watching cricket, leaving George to contemplate a soggy beermat. Every now and again George's eyes welled up with tears and the medieval monk smirking on the beermat turned into a shapeless brown splodge. He sniffed loudly, wiped his sleeve across his nose, and muttered to himself, 'Pull yourself together, you prat.'

But it was hard. George had seen a lot of accidents on the rigs, but that week he had witnessed one of the worst: he had been standing on the main deck, doing some routine welding, and suddenly he saw a massive wooden crate that was being loaded by a crane swing precariously out of control. It went hurtling through the air towards one of his oldest mates, Jim. George dropped his spanner and started to run across the deck, shouting at the top of his voice. But it was too late. He stopped dead in his tracks as he watched his friend's body being hurled through the air and smashed against the railings like a doll. Jim was crushed in a second.

At first, George had barely reacted to the accident at all. He didn't feel upset or even angry. He felt numb and started to wonder what was wrong with him. Was he really that heartless? But later, when he was watching TV in the lounge after supper, he was suddenly sick all over the floor. And ever since then, when he closed his eyes, he had a vision of Jim's battered, crumpled body hanging over the railings, limp and lifeless.

'Give us a refill, Bill,' George shouted through to the back room where Bill had fallen asleep in the armchair.

Bill eventually shuffled into the bar, yawning. 'Why don't you go home, George,' he said. 'You've had enough.'

'Last one.'

'It always is.'

Sheila didn't look up when she heard George crashing through the kitchen later that night. No need to wonder who was there. It was gone eleven and the twins had been dispatched to Nan's three hours earlier. The make-up she had carefully applied that morning had seeped into her pale, sallow skin and disappeared altogether. The lipstick was gone, smudged away by over a packet of cigarettes. Her face was drawn and tense.

Sheila wanted to pick up that TV and hurl it at George.

'Thanks a bundle for the welcome, you miserable old bag,' George muttered. He started to wobble as he staggered into the room and caught hold of the back of the sofa to steady himself.

Sheila gritted her teeth pretending, just for a moment, that he wasn't there.

He staggered over, bent down and looked into her face. A wave of alcoholic fumes were torpedoed out of his mouth when he said, 'You're a bundle of fun, you are.'

'Get away from me. You stink like an old skunk.'

'Oh . . . bollocks!' George staggered into the kitchen, hurled open the fridge door and reached inside for a can of beer.

'You're pissed enough as it is.'

'I've only had a couple.'

'Couple of barrels.'

George sat alone in the middle of the sofa, sulking like a naughty child. He was a big man—well over six feet tall—and had put on a few pounds over the years. His presence filled the living room almost entirely. He drained the can of beer, crushed it in his fist and chucked it into the waste-paper basket. Then he sighed, sat back, and started to feel guilty. He didn't know what to say. He knew he had behaved like a pig but he couldn't stop himself. He'd lost control. Again.

'If you weren't nagging every five minutes, I'd be back already,' he tried.

'Oh, shut up, for God's sake. How can I nag you when you're not even here?'

'All right. Well, I'm sorry. I didn't mean to.'

'You never do.'

'Yeah, well . . . you're not stuck out on that rig for two weeks at a time.'

'I suppose you think it's easy here? Left on my own with four children to look after.'

'What do they need you for? Even Bobby and Sue are at school full time.'

Sheila started to flick neurotically from one television channel to the next, lighting up one cigarette from the last. 'All you do on that rig of yours is work, eat, and sleep,' she said, trembling with rage. 'You've got nothing to worry about. You're well out of it. We could be dead for all you care. And then . . . you . . . you . . . you just . . . ' Sheila's frail body began to heave as she broke into tears.

'Come on, love. We're both tired.' George tried to touch his wife's shoulder. 'Let's call it a day and get to bed.'

'Get away from me, you mongrel,' she screamed. 'Get away.'

'OK, all you funkettes! We want to see you moooove!'

A handful of men stood around the bar, lifting their pints of beer mechanically to their mouths and looking blankly at the Rhythm Sisters. No interest registered.

'Wake up,' Sadie screamed at them.

No one batted an eyelid. They were only there for the beer. The Blue Dragon had an extension that night and as soon as the other pubs shut everyone would make their way over to the dingy back hall for some late-night drinking. The fact that the Rhythm Sisters were there too was totally incidental.

Sadie carried on regardless. She ignored them. In her mind she was playing to thousands at Wembley. She was Madonna. Or Annie Lennox. Anyone really. Except her.

'On the drums, we have . . . Aaaarabella!' she yelled.

Arabella crashed out a drum roll and then smashed her sticks violently on to the cymbals.

'And on sax . . . Liiiiiiiiz Dean!'

Liz launched into the first few bars of 'Summertime'. She tried to ignore the audience, seeing as they were ignoring her, but it was hard. Embarrassing really.

After the gig everyone was disappointed. As the girls loaded their equipment into Arabella's 'van'—a 1950s hearse that had been painted mauve—there was a subdued, anti-climactic feeling in the early morning air.

'It was like playing in a vacuum.'

'They could have been dead.'

'I thought they were.'

'That git at the front was driving me mad. Shouting out like that. He sounded bloody mad.'

'Dirty bastard.'

'Of course Cas never came.' Arabella turned the gum in her mouth around and around. She had to. Otherwise she spoke too posh. Being the wayward daughter of a high court judge wasn't easy; she had standards to live down to; ear-rings to tend to, lots of them, running down both ear lobes, plus a couple more in her nose. Her boyfriend, Cas, had just come out of prison and used Arabella's flat like a hotel, turning up when he felt like it. Of course, Arabella adored him.

'Just look at it like another practice session. The more we get the better.'

'Yeah. Only three weeks to go, girls. Don't forget.'

Liz dumped the last speaker on to the rusty floor of Arabella's hearse, stood up and stretched. She was tired. It was almost two in the morning and the air was hot and clammy. She wished she could take a shower and just flop into bed, right there and then. But Boughton was a twenty-mile drive away and she had to stay awake. She turned her head and looked for the hundredth time at the posters which lined the inside of the hearse:

THE TOWN & COUNTRY CLUB
PROUDLY PRESENTS
Dave Arnold
The Rhythm Sisters
The Linda Belinda Double Act
and
Greased Lightning
in a Grand Evening Spectacular

Liz grinned. 'Three weeks,' she said to herself. Three weeks to the big night. That was all they had to prepare for the most important event, ever. Their big chance. Chance of a lifetime. Everyone would be there: people from the music business, managers, scouts—all sniffing around for new talent. Of course, the place would be packed. It always was. It was the most exclusive venue in Norfolk. Posters were up and the word was out. Liz went all wobbly every time she saw one.

'Hey, what's a "grand evening spectacular"?' she shouted to Sadie.

'Us!' Sadie yelled back.

'Just shut it, will you,' the publican hissed from the bar window. 'I don't need any more complaints about the noise.'

Liz knew George was home because she could hear him snoring in her parents' bedroom. The noise reverberated around the house like a threat, hounding every corner.

Before going to her own room, Liz opened the door of the twins' room. Both beds were empty. They had been taken round to Nan and Dad's. That was the drill: if George didn't show up by eight o'clock in the evening, Sheila, with a face like a sour lemon, would silently bundle them into the back of the Vauxhall and drive them round. Both Bobby and Sue would slump back into the seat in silence, their grazed legs dangling over the edge, and Bobby's thumb firmly planted in his mouth. Sue had developed eczema on her hands and sat mutely scratching her raw bleeding fingers as they jolted along in the car. They both knew and didn't know what was going on. They felt fear. But they didn't know why.

Without waiting to be asked, Liz got up the next morning and drove around to her grandparents who lived in a small fisherman's cottage on the sea front. Reluctantly, and only on the promise of an ice cream when they got back, the twins clambered into the car. But when they got home, they sank into a heavy mood of despondency and walked around the house on tiptoe because George was still asleep. They could hear his snoring and grunting as he hurled himself around in bed. No one dared move or speak or hardly breathe. Even when he was asleep, he took over the whole house.

When George got up, the first thing he did was to stroll down to the town and buy Sheila a large bunch of flowers. 'There you go, love. Sorry I was such a pain last night.'

She accepted them grudgingly. Every time they had a row, he'd turn up with something. She got fed up with it. They could put the money to better use.

In the afternoon, George flopped into his armchair and started zapping the remote control at the TV, racing from channel to channel. When Liz walked in, he looked up, surprised. 'Oh, it's you,' he grunted.

Liz ignored him. George didn't know how to greet anyone cheerfully or pay a compliment; he thought they'd take advantage—of what, no one knew. 'Get your sax out and we'll have a blast?' he said, turning the TV off and chucking the remote control on the floor.

That was a surprise. George rarely played the trumpet any more. The battered black case he kept it in had become a coffin. The most he ever did these days was to get out the instrument and polish it. And neither did he listen to his old LPs. His famous collection had sat gathering dust in the corner for years. Now all he did was sit in front of the telly.

Liz started to feel uncomfortable and squirmed by the door. 'Can't, Dad,' she said nervously. 'I've got to practise for the concert.'

'Show us the music and I'll practise with you.'

'It's a solo.'

'Oh, well, bloody charming,' George snapped, angrily getting out of the chair. 'Remind me not to bother teaching you anything.'

'Well, there are some numbers we could play together,' Liz suggested, backing down. She hated herself for not standing up to her father, but she couldn't help it. As soon as she sensed his anger rising, she felt flooded by panic.

'That's big of you.' Furious, George pushed past her and stormed into the kitchen.

'Look, Dad, we could . . . '

'Forget it.'

'What about . . . '

'Just don't bloody bother. Anyway, I've got more than enough to do.'

A few minutes later, when George discovered everyone had gone out and he was alone in the house, on his first day back, he slammed the kettle down on to the oven in a fury. 'Bloody marvellous!' he shouted, and stormed off to the pub.

When Liz got to the other side of town, she turned off the main road and cycled along a small, grass-covered lane. She soon reached an old disused bridge which arched over one of the many sludgy estuaries winding in from the sea. There, she dropped her bike on to the dry, grassy bank.

Underneath the bridge, the air was thick and damp and had a slightly bitter, urinous smell. But the acoustics were superb. Liz took out her sax and began to play; the deep resonant notes echoed through the air, bathing her in sound, drowning her, washing through every cell of her body. She allowed herself to be transported into the future, to the Town and Country Club in three weeks' time. All eyes were on her as she played her own version of 'Stormy Weather'—solo. The audience was mesmerized. The talent scouts were scribbling madly in their notebooks. Her family was entranced; Sheila, Nan and Dad, Gary, and George who was grinning from ear to ear with pride. She shone like a glittering jewel. Even Arabella and Sadie were blown away and stood quite still during the complete performance.

Amanda Grimsby was walking along the dry, dusty road, her hands in her shorts pockets, her face slightly tilting upwards towards the sun. She could allow herself that luxury because she had smothered herself with factor 20 sun cream before she left home. She was only just seventeen, but well aware of the harmful effects of the sun.

She had had to get away from the house, to escape her mother's incessant talking. It drove her mad, especially when her father was away and she had to cope with it single-handed. In fact, 'it'—the talking—had got even worse since the family had moved to Boughton a few years ago. The Grimsbys just didn't fit in. They were too Surrey. Mrs Grimsby, or Sarah to the bridge crowd, put people off with her airs and graces and Guildford talk. She never stopped babbling. On and on she went, about nothing at all. Words spewed from her mouth like vomit, filling the unbearable silence. She couldn't help it, it was like a disease.

Amanda's father, Peter Grimsby, had hoped their smart new detached house might keep his wife happy. It was the sort of place she had always dreamed of but which they could never afford in the Home Counties. But the novelty of the house soon wore off—and the talk wore on. And then Mrs Grimsby's behaviour grew very strange because she had started to receive dirty phone calls every time Peter went off-shore to work on the rigs. It wasn't what the caller said that upset Mrs Grimsby, but the fact that he always knew when she was alone. After the last spate of calls, she had suddenly produced a shotgun and a wallet full of cartridges at the breakfast table.

Amanda pursed her lips and sighed deeply as she strode along the road towards the sea. It was all right for her father, he disappeared for half the year. She was the one who had to put up with her mother. Thank God she only had two more years at home before going to university.

As Amanda rounded a corner, she suddenly heard the muffled tones of a saxophone and strained her ears to detect where the sound was coming from.

After Liz had played for a good half hour, she wandered out into the sun, screwing up her eyes as they adjusted to the stark light of the day. Her neck was stiff; she rolled her head around and shrugged her shoulders several times. When she opened her eyes, she saw a girl lying on the river bank, pulling at long tufts of dry grass and squinting in her direction. 'Hope you don't mind,' said the girl. 'I was just walking along the lane and heard you playing.'

Liz raised her eyebrows. It was Amanda Grimsby. They had been in the same class at school but had nothing in common and hardly ever spoke to each other. Amanda loved school and Liz had hated it. Amanda had stayed on and Liz had left as soon as she could; 'Escape from Alcatraz,' she called it.

Liz smiled, chucked her leather jacket on to the grass and flopped on top of it.

Amanda nodded at the jacket. 'Looks a bit warm for this weather.'

Liz shrugged her shoulders. 'Not really.'

'Are you practising for the concert?' Amanda turned on to her stomach and started picking away at a bald patch of earth.

'How do you know about that?'

'I've got tickets. I'm coming with Jenny Murphy.'

'Oh?'

'Can't wait. We're all seething with envy.'

Liz couldn't imagine Amanda Grimsby being envious of anyone. She was one of those perfect creatures who always looked immaculate. Feminine. Sophisticated. Her blonde hair was cut in a bob and framed her smooth, tanned face. She was stylish but simple in her dress. She could throw on any old thing and look great. All the boys fancied her. But she always stuck to some boring-looking bloke she had been going out with for years and who was at university. He used to stay with the Grimsbys in their big posh house in St Margaret's Drive and meet Amanda from school in her father's car. In Liz's view, anyone that acceptable to parents had to be a major drag.

'Is your father home?' Amanda asked.

'He got back last night.'

'I wish mine was around. He might get my mother off my back. She's been driving me crazy.'

Liz raised her eyebrows. She couldn't share Amanda's enthusiasm for having her father home. But then their fathers were totally different: they both worked off-shore on the rigs, but were worlds apart. To start with, Liz's father, George, was a contract worker who could be hired and fired at a second's notice; whereas Amanda's father was a company man, a fully qualified engineer with job security, a pension and a list of perks as long as your arm. Both girls were well aware of the differences, but they said nothing. They didn't have to. It was all so obvious. Amanda lived in St Margaret's Drive, a tree-lined avenue where large houses owned by oil executives and wealthy solicitors were distanced from the road by several acres of manicured lawn. Liz lived in a semi-detached council house down the Harborough Road. The Grimsbys had a Volvo Estate sitting in the driveway, whilst the Deans made do with a clapped-out old Vauxhall which overheated when it went faster than 50 mph. The Grimsbys went abroad at least twice a year; Liz had never left the country.

Liz wasn't envious. But she knew Amanda somehow felt

she had to apologize for being born into a more materialistically privileged family.

'When do you think noise becomes music?' Amanda asked, changing the subject and rolling over to face the sun.

'When do blobs become art?'

'Mmmm.' Amanda thought about this for a moment as she watched the seagulls gliding through the sky above them. 'I learnt to play the piano years ago,' she said. 'But I wasn't any good. Haven't got the ear.'

'You're good at everything else,' said Liz.

'I'm not. I'm a Jack-of-all-trades. Mediocre. Average at lots of things. I'd rather be like you.'

Even though Liz didn't believe her, she blushed and said nothing at first. 'No, you wouldn't,' she eventually replied.

Amanda turned over, rested her head in her hands and stared at Liz without saying anything. 'Can I come again?' she asked.

Liz blushed again. 'If you want.'

After a few days, George emerged from his coma. At first he was like a shaky animal, then he started to get restless. He was like an irritable mongoose that growled and gnashed around all day and could never get settled. Everyone pretended to ignore him, but the house revolved around him. It was always the same.

Sheila begrudged George's very existence. The fact that he even arrived at the house twice a month expecting to be let in, to be welcomed, infuriated her. He didn't do anything in particular to annoy her. He was just there. He was just him. George.

All day he sat in that armchair in front of the telly. When he hauled himself up, he either went for a pee, to eat at the kitchen table, or to the fridge where he would help himself to another can of beer.

'You've worn a path in the carpet. Between that chair and the fridge.'

'So? It's my bloody carpet.'

He had to remind her. Had to tell her that even though *she* had spent the past twenty years keeping the house together, everything in it belonged to *him*. She wanted to scream. She wanted to throttle him. Strangle him. Beat him to a pulp. But she didn't. She didn't because at the end of the day it *was* his carpet and there was nothing she could do about it.

The kids—Gary, Liz, Bobby and Sue—had their own methods of keeping out of their father's way. When one of them saw George lolloping down the road towards the house, he or she would give one whistle if he was coming round the back and two whistles for the front. Then they'd charge out of whichever door he wasn't coming through.

Gary had always taken the brunt of his father's temper. George couldn't stand him. 'Namby-pamby,' he called him. 'Put some bloody backbone into it, for God's sake,' he would yell, watching his son grapple with chopping logs for firewood. 'Look. Watch me.' George snatched the axe from Gary and wielded it high in the air, bringing it down with a ferocious blow and smashing the log into splinters. Gary jerked back in terror. 'Big girl's blouse,' George snarled throwing the axe back at Gary.

Sometimes, when George got really drunk, he ripped a rod from the staircase and beat his son with it. 'Act like a man!' he bellowed, almost frothing at the mouth as he watched Gary cower in the corner of the hall, covering his head with his arms, a low wail squeezing itself out from him. 'Come on. Fight. Fight back for once.'

Of course, George was all remorse and watery smiles the next day, but it was too late by then. Everyone tried to forgive, but they couldn't. Not really.

On his fifth night back, George woke up covered in sweat and grappling with the blankets. He had had the same nightmare for days: he opens the door to one of the storerooms on the rig and sees Jim Drew's head sitting in a bucket, grinning at him.

'Not again,' Sheila murmured, heaving the covers back to her side of the bed. 'What's the matter with you?'

'Nothing,' George grunted, his heart pounding.

'You ought to go and see a doctor. Something's not right.'

George couldn't tell Sheila about Jim Drew. Or what it was like seeing his friend's head sitting in that bucket. She wouldn't want to know anyway. She would never understand what it was like working on the rigs.

'What sort of places are those rigs for someone to spend half his life on?' George shouted, slamming his empty beer mug on the bar of the Crown and Anchor.

'Don't ask me,' Bill replied. 'And if you did, I'd say you were all bloody mad anyway.'

'Don't ask me why I do it. Just don't bloody ask.'

'Go on then.'

'For them of course. That's why. And what happens? I come back. Ask for a few home comforts. And then what? Nothing. They don't want to know. No one does. I might as well be the invisible bloody man in that house.'

'You'd have a job.'

When George left the Crown and Anchor, he made his way along the coast road which ran between the sea and a terrace of small fishermen's cottages. Nan and Dad lived at the end of the terrace near the boathouse which had been shut down a few years back and was now collapsing in on itself like a rotting skeleton.

Nan said the mice were coming over from the boathouse, but Dad said they had always been there and that Nan was getting senile.

Nan and Dad had three children: George was the eldest, Mavis was number two, and Arthur was 'the baby' and still living at home, aged thirty-seven. As usual, when George arrived, he had to clamber over a partially dismantled Bantum motor bike which Arthur was continually pulling apart and putting back together again. 'Never seen you ride the bugger once,' Dad always grumbled. 'Thought you might ride away on it one day and stop scrounging off us all the time.'

'Oh shut up, you,' said Nan. 'I don't want to be left on my own with you in this house. It's miserable enough as it is.'

Dad sniffed and allowed a long stringy strand of snot to fall on to his grubby shirt.

That was the afternoon Dad announced that he and Nan were thinking of adopting a baby.

George and Arthur were shovelling one of Nan's famed 'snacks' down themselves at the time: sausage, egg, bacon, mashed potato, and gallons of tea which she always milked and sugared in the pot. They stopped eating, looked at each other blankly, and then went back to their tea. 'Don't be daft,' Arthur finally drawled. 'You're too old.'

'I don't see why,' Dad replied. 'We've got the experience. Three of you lot.'

'You're too old,' said George. 'They wouldn't even give you a second look.'

Dad's face crinkled up like an old leaf. He looked at Nan, his tired yellow eyes droopy and sad. It was as they expected, as they knew. But, for a while, he and his old wife had allowed themselves to be swept along by the fantasy of having another 'young un' around the house.

'Well, there's the Africans,' Nan said. 'You know, the ones you see on the news. They need looking after too.'

'It's the same.' Arthur smirked sideways at George.

'You're a glutton for punishment, the both o' yer,' George chipped in, trying to humour his parents. 'You've got enough with him, haven't you?' George nodded at Arthur. 'He'll never flee the nest, that one.'

Later on, after tea, Arthur disappeared back to his motor bike and George flopped into Nan's armchair in front of the telly. Nan sat perched on one of the dining chairs and began to fiddle around with some darning.

Then Alice Murdoch popped in with some photographs. Her dog had died a couple of weeks ago and she had pictures of him lying mottled and mangy in a small wooden coffin.

'He does look peaceful,' said Nan. 'You gave him a good send off, Alice.'

'He went in his sleep.'

'Best way.'

'How we'd all like to go.'

'And that's a dear little coffin.'

'Herbie made it. We've actually had it some time, waiting, you know. But we never wanted Benjy to see it. We kept it up in the roof.'

Nan nodded knowingly.

'Of course, I did the lining and the trim,' Alice went on, tracing the outline of the coffin on the photo with her chipped nail.

Suddenly George let out a huge dramatic sigh, pulled himself out of the chair and strode towards the door. The two women looked up in alarm at his sudden, violent movement. 'Where are you off to, then?' Nan asked.

'To the only place in this poxy town where there's any sanity.'

3

Two weeks until the big night. Two weeks to pull a rag-tag of a band together and create a noise that sounded just a little like everyone was playing the same tune at the same time.

When they formed the band, the Rhythm Sisters had just got together for the fun of it. They never expected anyone to take them seriously. And then suddenly they were offered a gig at the Town and Country Club. And panicked.

They practised in a huge, falling-down warehouse which had been converted into scores of glorified cubicles that were rented out as 'workshops' or 'offices'. And because the warehouse stood next to the canal, it stank like rotting sewage, especially down in the basement which reeked of damp, even in summer.

When Liz walked into the studio, Arabella was setting up her drums. 'Oh, it's you,' she said as though she had been expecting someone else.

'Glad you're so pleased to see me.'

'Sadie's late. Of course.' Arabella sniffed loudly and shuffled over to a chair, barely lifting her feet which had been encased in big black biker boots ever since Liz had known her. When she reached the chair, she sniffed again, chucked her dyed red hair over her shoulder, and started gnawing on a half-eaten croissant.

'The studio' was down in the basement and sound-proofing was basic: the walls and ceiling were lined with tatty sheets of cork and pieces of old carpet which were covered with graffiti. The floor was covered with other bits of threadbare carpet which were totally pox-ridden and speckled with hundreds of black cigarette burns. Large black speakers sat on milk crates and a tangle of wires seethed around the floor like snakes, linking the instruments to the amplifiers and the amplifiers to the speakers.

Sadie was always late. She couldn't help it. She couldn't wait for anything; if she had five minutes to spare she would go off on a shopping spree or drop in on a friend, so she always ended up late after all. When she eventually rushed in through the studio door, she said a woman had been run over in the High Street and held up the buses. She always had some huge excuse. Sadie's life was full of drama.

'You should write a book of excuses,' Arabella grumbled. 'It would get to the top of the fiction charts.'

Sadie sneered and then started pouting into the microphone, making all sorts of huffing and blowing noises before she started to tune her guitar. Then she took a slurp of water and said, 'My throat's bloody killing me.' Liz and Arabella rolled their eyes and made faces at each other while they waited.

'One, two, three, four'—Arabella knocked her drumsticks together and off they went; thumping and crashing, Sadie leaping up and down on the floor, Arabella bouncing around behind the drums like a chimpanzee, sweat pouring down her face, the muscles on her arms rippling through her pale, almost translucent, flesh. And Liz grabbed the microphone to do backing vocals when she wasn't playing the sax.

On and on they went. Over and over the same numbers. Again and again. Until they got it at least half-way there. And then they'd drink more water and smoke more cigarettes. Then try it a different way and a different way and a different way, playing the original sound track over and over again on Sadie's clapped out old tape recorder.

'Why can't we just slow it down?'

'It won't work.'

'Then let's just end with three full choruses and cut.'

'Try A minor and F first and then on to E for the second chorus.'

'That doesn't work.'

'Then let's go back to E.'

'I said it was E in the first place.'

'No, you didn't. You wanted to try F.'

'That's not what . . . '

'Oh, shut up. Come on. Let's just do it.'

The night wore on. Scores of cigarettes burnt themselves out on rusty old tin ashtrays, water became tepid and stale, coffee formed skins and grew cold in mugs. The air became so thick with smoke the girls could barely see each other.

The noise vibrated through their whole bodies, through the studio, the launderette upstairs, the offices and workshops. Six hours passed unnoticed. And when they eventually staggered out of the studios dripping in sweat and exhausted, the silence was almost deafening.

When Liz got home later that evening, Sheila was pacing around the house chain-smoking.

'What's the matter?' Liz asked, dropping her sax on the sofa and flopping down next to it.

'It's your dad.' Sheila sat down, lit another cigarette, and then got up again. 'Something's happened.'

Liz didn't ask what. She sat, waiting patiently. Anything could have happened. She was used to it.

'There's been a fight.'

'Where?'

'Down the Crown and Anchor.' More pacing from Sheila, she inhaled deeply on the cigarette and blew the smoke out into the room like a fire-eater. 'He's been arrested.'

Liz sighed deeply and began to play around with the zip on her sax case.

'I don't know why. It was only a disagreement. You'd think they had better things to do.'

'Who?'

'The police.'

'Where is he now?'

'Norwich. In the nick.' Sheila was pale. Her whole body was shaking and rattling as though it might collapse into a heap of bones at any minute. 'I don't know,' she said. 'Now what are we meant to do?'

'Same as we always do,' said Liz standing up. 'Nothing. I'm going to bed.'

'I was helpless because you had the car.'

'Well, I didn't know . . . '

Suddenly Sheila turned, looked wildly at Liz and said, 'I'd better go and see him.'

'They won't let you. They never do.'

'I'd better be there. You know what he's like. At least if I'm there he can't complain.'

'About what?'

'About not getting any support.'

'It's not your fault. You didn't have anything to do with it.'

'Try telling him that.'

Liz started to wander into the hall. 'Want me to drive you?'

'No. Someone's got to look after the twins. And where's Gary?' Suddenly Sheila remembered Gary, her first born, who seemed to have evaporated from her life. Suddenly, in all this confusion and drama, she thought of him.

'I don't know.'

'He's never around. Treats the place like a hotel. I can hardly remember what he looks like any more. Probably pass him in the street without recognizing him.'

'Try talking to him one day.'

'He's never here to talk to.'

And then, as if to cue, Liz and Sheila saw the long, cheerless profile of Gary pass the kitchen window. His head looked as though it was on a stick. Liz and Sheila glanced at each other, surprised, and then watched him slouch through the kitchen like a shadow, his shoulders hunched forward, his hands sunk deep into his pockets, his stare firmly fixed to the floor as he negotiated his way across the worn lino.

'Where do you think you're going?' Sheila suddenly shouted as he disappeared into the hallway. Gary stopped, quite still. He didn't move. He didn't speak. All you could see were the knobbles of his vertebrae sticking out through his T-shirt. 'Sit down,' Sheila ordered.

Gary backtracked a few steps and sat down. His hands remained in his pockets, his long lanky legs were awkwardly pulled up under the table. He waited.

'Now I don't want you breathing a word of this,' Sheila started, leaning against the sink, folding her arms and looking down at her son, 'but your father's been taken in again.'

'I know,' Gary mumbled.

'How do you know?'

'The whole town knows. He had a scrap with Roger Drain.'

'What about?'

'I don't know. Cards, I think.'

'Well, what about them?'

'He accused Roger of cheating.'

Sheila didn't say anything. She sighed, stared ahead, and then disappeared into her thoughts and completely forgot about Gary and Liz. Gary waited a little longer, then peeled himself off the plastic kitchen chair and wandered off. Sheila didn't seem to notice he had gone.

After Liz had seen Sheila splutter off down the road in the Vauxhall, she heard Bobby and Sue scamper back to their beds upstairs; they had watched the great departure from their bedroom window. When Liz went up to see what was going on, she overheard Sue say in a schoolmarmish voice, 'Now then, Bobby, you really must go to sleep. You've got school tomorrow.'

Sheila spent the whole night sitting on the hard bench of the police station waiting room, propped up against the wall. The next morning, George made a brief and shamefaced appearance in the magistrates court, was fined £100 and bound over to keep the peace. He and Sheila drove back to Boughton together, neither saying a single word during the complete journey. George kept his stare firmly fixed to the road and Sheila looked out of the window, yet saw nothing. When they arrived back at the house they were greeted by a pair of transparent white rubber gloves hanging up above the sink. Sheila groaned, 'Oh no, not her,' and then stormed off up to the bedroom where she slammed the door and threw herself on the bed.

While George was standing alone in the kitchen, Nan bustled in. 'You're back, then,' she muttered, picking up the remains of the children's dishes and plonking them in the sink. 'Don't need to ask where you've been, of course.'

'Don't then,' George growled, sitting down and pushing his large hands through his hair.

'The whole town knows.'

George ignored her. He felt awful; his eyes were bloodshot, his mouth felt like sandpaper and he had a thick coat of stubble on his face. Suddenly Bobby charged down the stairs and into the kitchen. When he saw George, he stopped, looked at his father, wide-eyed and terrified, searching his face for clues as to what sort of mood he was in. And then he just ran away, without saying a word. George watched him and suddenly felt overwhelmed with sadness that his own son should be too afraid to go anywhere near him. He threw his head into his hands and let out a long sigh.

'Would have thought you'd have grown out of all that by now,' said Nan who was gloved and beginning to attack the washing up. 'Scrapping in the pub. That's the sort of behaviour I wouldn't even expect from Gary.'

'Of course you wouldn't from that nancy boy,' George mumbled.

'Leave him alone, you bully you. Just because he's not some great oaf don't mean to say he's no good.' Nan had a soft spot for Gary. She felt sorry for the boy. 'You could be a lot nicer to him, you could,' she added as she plunged her hands into the soapy hot water.

George ignored her and stood up, noisily scraping the chair against the floor.

'I'm going to get some kip.'

That morning, Muriel Drain had been round at Nan's cottage, in the taxi, at eight o'clock sharp. She had been up since six thirty taking men to the heliport and then mooched around the sea front, itching and twitching, waiting for a decent hour when she could drop round to Nan's and accidentally-on-purpose break the news about George. The pretext she visited Nan on was chickens: Florrie Dobbs had some very tender young pullets for sale and would Nan be interested?

'Dead or alive?' Nan frowned suspiciously at Muriel as she pulled off her rubber gloves. Something was up, she knew. She didn't believe for one minute that Muriel Drain was round at that hour just to sell her a chicken.

'Either,' said Muriel, knowing for a fact that the chickens were live. Florrie insisted they still had plenty of go in them and were 'bootiful layers'.

As it happened, Nan was having 'a lunch' on Sunday because George was going off-shore again the following day. A nice chicken would have suited her perfectly. 'I might be interested in a dead one,' she said, slanting her head slightly and looking at Muriel from the corner of her eye.

Muriel's attention had wandered away from Nan and she was looking up the hallway, trying to piece together the bits of Arthur's motor bike in her imagination. She was quickly pulled back into the conversation by Nan, who suddenly snapped, 'For a price.'

‘Righto then,’ said Muriel and began to back away. And just as she was about to turn and make her way back to the taxi, she said, ‘And how long do you reckon they’ll keep George in, then?’

That was it. What Nan had been waiting for. She looked at Muriel, without flinching, and said, ‘For a price, remember.’

There had been a time when Nan had been able to rely on Dad to feed her gossip from the town, but his visits to the Crown and Anchor were becoming few and far between. He simply wasn’t up to it any more; he’d more or less given up his bicycle altogether and, after thinking it through long and hard, he decided that a night of sitting in the pub just couldn’t justify the long trudge home any more. These days Dad preferred to stay put in front of the telly and had become addicted to all the soaps which he was always muddling up. He couldn’t understand why so-and-so was having another baby when she’d only had one two months ago, and what was that other so-and-so doing in the pub when he was meant to have emigrated to Australia?

When Liz wandered into the kitchen that morning, before George and Sheila arrived back from court, Nan was sitting at the table in her faded pinny rolling up small pieces of cardboard to put in the spouts of the teapots to stop dust getting in. How Nan hated dust. Since she was a small child she had spent almost her whole life in single-handed combat against it. ‘I suppose your mum’s been out all night?’ she said.

Liz grunted and wandered over to the sink to fill up the kettle. The last person she felt like seeing was Nan.

‘There was a time when at least you pretended to be pleased to see me,’ said Nan.

‘Sorry, Nan.’ Liz bent over and kissed the old woman’s sagging, wrinkled cheek. She felt sorry for Nan, but at the same time her grandmother got on her nerves; she was too naggy and fussy and insular. She was the sort of person people laughed at in the street, thinking she was a bit of a character. But she had spent her whole life in Boughton and didn't know how to be or behave in any other way. She didn't know any better. Liz hated that.

'I found a goldfish in the toilet this morning,' Nan said. 'Swimming around it was. Poor thing.'

'That's Bobby I expect. He did something funny like that last time there . . . there was some trouble.'

'I was just about to flush the chain.'

'What happened?'

'Fished it out, of course.' Nan nodded at a glass that was sitting on the window ledge; the goldfish was frantically swimming around and around, looking for a way out.

Liz grinned to herself and wondered how anything could survive for more than a few seconds in Nan's thick, yellow urine.

That morning Liz had planned to go down and practise under the bridge again. On the way, she passed Karen who was standing inside the bus shelter, done up to the nines and dressed in a short skirt and high heels. It was another hot and humid day and the rubbish which was embedded in the dark corners of the bus shelter stank. 'It stinks in there. How can you stand in it without being sick?' asked Liz.

'I'm used to stink,' said Karen angrily. 'I've got stink up to here.' And she thrust her hand across her forehead dramatically.

Liz dismounted her bicycle and squinted in Karen's direction. Even after a scorching summer, Karen was white. She had pale, see-through skin and dyed auburn hair. She never went out in the sun; if she did, she looked like a brandy snap after half an hour. Karen preferred to stay the same pallid colour all year round and always wore the same clothes whatever the season; skimpy tops and short skirts—all carefully selected from mail-order catalogues. Even in winter she never wore tights. Her goosey legs turned a bluish colour and went all blotchy with cold. Comfort didn't matter to Karen. Appearance was everything—though no one would have thought it.

'I don't want to talk about it.' Karen looked away from Liz and pursed her lips tighter, tighter. Then suddenly she spluttered into great sobs. 'If you get asked out, you at least expect them to turn up. Don't you? I mean, don't you? Why ask someone out, if you've got no intention of showing up?' Karen wasn't waiting for an answer. She picked away nervously at the cuticles of her nails, several of which were bleeding.

'Who was it, then?'

'You'd never believe it if I told you.'

Liz raised her eyebrows and tilted her head sideways.

Karen looked down at her white stilettos and bit her lip. 'Mutley,' she yelled. 'Mutley, for Christ's sake! Can you believe it? He asked me out after he gave me a lift into Norwich the other day.'

Karen then went quiet and dropped her head in disgrace, diverting her attention back to her bleeding cuticles. 'As if anyone would want to go out with him anyway,' she muttered.

Liz didn't say anything. She looked at Karen and felt sorry for her: What was it like to live without hope? Without a dream? To pin your future on finding some bloke? On getting married. And then what? When she had that man. What would she do then?

Neither girl said anything for a moment. No one was around. Normally, at this time of day, the High Street was buzzing with holiday-makers stocking up with provisions, but they'd all gone home. The air hung stagnant and still, churned only by insects which buzzed around the rubbish, making the occasional foray into Karen's hair.

Suddenly the girls saw Roger Drain appear from the taxi office and disappear into the Crown and Anchor. Not being able to drive any more was a blessing in disguise, he could drink as much as he wanted without feeling a scrap of guilt. Even in that heat he was wearing the old brown cardigan his mother had knitted him fifteen years ago. He never took it off. It stank of him, stank of Roger Drain concentrate.

'I never trust men who wear cardigans,' Karen mumbled.

'Didn't think you were that fussy.'

'Thanks.'

'Sorry. Only a joke. Didn't mean it. Really.'

The next practice session did not go well. Sadie and Arabella had had a row because Arabella had introduced a record producer to the band and Sadie ended up going out on a date with him. After a disastrous session, Arabella and Sadie sat in the pub and wouldn't look each other in the eye. They silently snorted and sulked like horses. Arabella shoved her Doc Martens up on the bench looking nonchalantly around her as she twiddled a row of gold earrings and Sadie sat staring sulkily into her drink.

'I don't know what you're so pissed off about,' Sadie finally grumbled. 'You wouldn't be able to go out with him anyway.'

'Who says?'

'What about Cas?'

'What about him. He doesn't own me.' Arabella sniffed loudly and opened a tin of tobacco.

'I can't see what's wrong with Sadie going out with him,' said Liz, fed up with the whole situation.

'Who asked you?' Arabella lit a roll-up and threw the matches across the table in frustration. She was fed up with the stinking group anyway. She should go solo, but who wanted to listen to a solo drummer? She'd have to learn to play the guitar. Then she wouldn't need anyone.

4

The day before George was due to go back off-shore was a Sunday and so Nan had one of her lunches. She always granted every departure great ceremony, as though her first-born son was about to set sail around the world and might never return. Nan didn't know much about the rigs but she had spent her life watching men put out to sea in fishing trawlers and never come back. The fact that Dad was still around was a miracle. She never expected him to be, never thought she'd be stuck with him forever.

The chicken Muriel Drain promised had failed to materialize so Nan had to make do with a boiler instead. 'Of course, it's not the same as the real thing,' she grumbled as Dad stabbed away at the anaemic-looking creature. 'These factory birds taste like blotting paper. They've got no taste. No taste at all.'

'Since when have you ever eaten blotting paper?' George drawled grumpily.

'In America they breed them without feathers,' said Arthur.

'They don't.'

'They do. Saves plucking.'

Everyone at the table went quiet as they thought of naked chickens, clucking and fussing around like Nan.

'But how do they keep warm?' asked Bobby, banging the end of his knife on the table.

'They don't need to. Not when they're reared in a factory.'

Bobby curled his top lip, pushed his spoon around the

table like a racing car and then slyly looked up to see who was watching him. No one was very interested, they were all in a trance, mesmerized by Dad tearing at the chicken with his old carving knife and fork which he could barely keep a grip of. Bored, Bobby went back to his spoon and made a low, growling noise with his throat. Sitting next to him was Sue who sat bolt upright like Little Miss Muffet, her thin mousy hair dragged back into a pony-tail and her pale blue eyes staring vacantly at the bowl of peas before her. She didn't move. She didn't speak. She had to be good. And then everything would be all right.

'Who wants a beer?' Arthur scraped his chair back and lolloped off into the kitchen. 'George?'

George sat looking downcast, turning his glass around in his hand. He grunted.

'Don't we get asked, then?' Sheila shouted from the table. 'Anyone would have thought no one else existed in this world except you two.' Sheila sat back in her chair and from the corner of her eye cast a furtive look at Nan because the remark had been directly aimed at her. But Nan was far too preoccupied with Dad and the chicken.

'Put the spoon down, Bobby, and shut up. You're getting on everyone's nerves,' Sheila snapped.

'Your nerves, more like,' said George.

'Oh, shut up you too.'

Arthur returned with the beer and slammed a can down in front of George and another in front of Sheila. 'I didn't say I *wanted* one,' Sheila said. 'It would be nice to be asked, that's all.' She looked down at her hands which were rough and stained having spent the entire week installing a new bathroom suite.

'Oh, Christ!' Arthur sighed, took the can away and put it by his own place setting.

The meal proceeded. They all sat there, stuffing in food, sniffing and snorting, barely saying a word because no one had anything to say.

'What's the matter with you, Liz?' said Nan. 'You

haven't eaten a thing and you're looking more scrawny than that boiler.'

Liz shrugged her shoulders and said she wasn't hungry. She couldn't stand those lunches. Sitting there watching them all stuffing their faces like geese. No one said anything and yet everyone screamed venom at each other, silently. The atmosphere was so thick it was stifling. It was like dying of asphyxiation, slowly.

Although George's 'incident' was not mentioned, it soured the atmosphere like a bad hangover. Arthur couldn't resist the odd dig. 'I don't know what's happened to the youth of today—or any other generation, come to think of it,' he said, smirking and loading up his fork with more food. Dad, of course, was very upset about the whole thing. Nan had hoped he might not find out at all, seeing that he went into town so infrequently. But he had decided to hobble down to the hardware store one lunchtime and, sure enough, Will Carlton couldn't keep his trap shut for a minute. It quite upset Dad when he heard. When he returned, his face was pale and his body was shaking. At first Nan thought it was the strain of the walk home, but she soon found out the real reason.

And this wasn't the first time it had happened. George had already spent one night in the slammer and Arthur had been sent to a detention centre for six months when he was sixteen for stealing mopeds. Dad hadn't brought his sons up to scrap and fight in bars like big kids, steal what didn't belong to them, and behave like a couple of yobs. He had never done a dishonest deed in his life, apart from under-declaring his catch to the Inland Revenue from time to time, and that, he reckoned, was fair game.

Dad had always been disappointed neither of his sons had followed him to sea. Ten days rocking around the North Sea, cooped up in a cramped, damp trawler would have straightened them out in no time. In those conditions you had to learn to get on with others. There was no fighting allowed. No stealing. At least George had almost gone to sea. Arthur hadn't even made it off-shore; he had a semi job at a local garage where he would turn up when he felt like it and tinker around with cars between drinking hundreds of cups of tea. His boss said he'd only pay him by the hour because he was never in. Arthur had shrugged his shoulders and scooped a tea bag out of the oily mug. He didn't care.

'If they still had National Service none of this would have happened,' Dad suddenly spluttered half-way through lunch.

'Oh, God. Here we go again.'

'That'd knock the corners off yer. Teach you how to behave decently, like everyone used to. Like proper men.' The old man sat back in his chair and wiped his tired, yellow eyes with the back of his hand. He looked at his two sons. What a lot, he thought. What a lot they are. It's like being landed with a bad bloody job lot.

Everyone was beginning to worry that Dad was going a bit senile. Some days he was fine, on others he couldn't find his way around the house and Nan found him wandering around the back yard looking for the sink or the telly. Joseph, his brother who had died five years ago, suddenly started to make a miraculous comeback. In fact, these days, Dad talked to him more than he talked to anyone else.

And when he was tired, Dad sometimes didn't know who people were at all. You could see his mind whirling as he sat staring at Sheila, or even Arthur, wondering who the hell they were and what they were doing sitting at his table. After 'the incident' with George, Dad almost completely retreated into another world. 'Bloody wasters,' he mumbled to himself at the table.

'Shut up, Dad,' Nan snapped without looking up from her plate. She and Dad never looked at each other when they spoke. They didn't need to. After all these years they had their own shorthand, a tacit understanding which made words totally redundant.

'Well, I've got to go. Joseph needs a hand with scraping down the marshmallows . . . '

Bobby started to snigger. Sue kicked him under the table, maintaining her prim demeanour, though she wanted to laugh too. She wanted to scream.

'I said shut up.' Nan couldn't stand watching her husband slowly fade away. She felt as though he were leaving her. Even though he was still there in body, he was disappearing in mind and even spirit. She hated to see him 'act up with his nonsense' in front of others. She could almost make sense of his ramblings, turn them around so they didn't seem so strange. But when she watched other people's reactions there was no denying that her husband was losing his mind. 'No one wants to listen to your rantings.' Nan stuck a couple of fat fingers in her mouth and fished around for a stringy piece of chicken which had become lodged in her dentures.

Dad shut up for a moment and the whole family continued eating. No one talked. The only sound was of knives and forks tap dancing with each other, going clickety click and screeching and skidding across Nan's best china. After the last morsel of treacle pudding had been scraped from the inside of Nan's best blue bowl, Liz announced that she had to go. George looked up in surprise. 'Where?' he demanded.

'Work. I'm doing afternoon teas at the hotel,' said Liz getting up. 'And then I'm going out.'

'Where?' George snapped again.

'Out.'

'Out where?'

'What's it to you?'

'Talk to me like that and you're not going anywhere.'

Liz pursed her lips and glared at her father. She felt she hated him. 'I'm going out with the band,' she said.

'You make sure you're back by ten, otherwise there'll be trouble.'

Liz didn't reply. She bent down to give Nan a big kiss on

the cheek. 'Thanks, Nan. It was great.'

'Just a minute,' Nan said, slowly hauling herself up from her chair. 'Give us a hand with those plates before you go.'

Instinctively Sheila started to get up too, but Nan put her hand out to stop her. 'Not you. Liz and I can manage.' Sheila pursed her lips and sat down again, cross.

As Liz carried a stack of bowls out of the front room, she stuck her tongue out at Arthur who was leering at her as usual. When she got to the kitchen, which was always freezing whatever the season, Nan beckoned her over to a row of shelves where hundreds of china ornaments and teapots stood. Nan was obsessed with these little knick-knacks: thatched cottages, figurines of shepherdesses, lambs, cats, owls, Dick Whittingtons, Tom Thumbs—all in the worst possible taste. She snapped them up wherever she went and called them her 'dear little friends'. The window sill of the front room was covered with them. Liz often saw people looking at them; some sniggered, others admired.

Nan stretched to the top shelf and carefully lifted down a green teapot in the shape of a thatched cottage. She lifted the roof and with much puffing and panting, dipped her knobbly old fingers in as far as they would go, eventually pulling out a large wad of cash. Nan and Dad did not believe in banks. They paid for everything with cash and had never been in debt in their lives. The idea of owing money terrified them. It had taken Dad years to retire because he couldn't stand the idea of not being able to earn money any more. What if they needed a new roof one day? What if the house suddenly got dry rot? Or they suddenly got a big bill which swallowed up the savings? What if? What if? They lived their lives around 'what-ifs.'

Nan carefully pulled out a £10 note and gave it to Liz. 'Off you go, then,' she said.

Down on the river small boats were tacking up-stream making their way laboriously towards their moorings after a hard day's sailing. The tide was drawing back as though a plug had been pulled and, as the water withdrew, it left behind it long stretches of rich, brown mud which glistened in the last of the evening light. There was no noise except for the constant tinkling of the boat's rigging and the gentle lap of the waves as they folded into the shore like reams of silky fabric.

Amanda sat on a grassy bank, her legs pulled up. She had been there for some time and hardly noticed the evening begin to get colder. She had goose bumps on her arms, but she didn't notice that either. She simply stared at the river, feeling the sun disappear behind her, leaving her more and more in the dark with her thoughts. She took a deep breath and ran her hands down her face in despair as she thought of her life and how everything had so suddenly changed in the past twenty-four hours. Before, everything had seemed so certain, so sure. Now, she didn't know any more. Anything could happen. She leaned back in the grass and watched a flock of gulls circle the darkening sky above her. Soon she would be going back to school. Next year she was meant to be sitting her A levels. Would she get that far? Was university still a possibility? A career in law? Her dreams were slithering out of her grasp and evaporating into thin air. She didn't know how to grab them back. Didn't know what to do or where to go or who to ask for help. For the first time in her life she felt totally alone.

Amanda had no idea that a few yards away Liz was sitting in The Peg and Sail with Snot, Karen, and Mutley. Liz had lied to George about who she was seeing, she didn't see why she should answer to him. As usual Karen was dressed in a mini-skirt and high heels, while Snot and Mutley slouched around making stupid jokes and trying to impress the girls with their non-existent pool-playing skills. Liz picked up her beer and wandered out of the pub to take a breath of fresh air. By now the moon was shining; it lit a rough pathway which led down to the river and which was partly obscured by great sheaths of wiry grass that had flopped over it, exhausted by the relentless summer. Liz felt slightly drunk. She wasn't used to drinking and a pint of beer sent her head spinning. As she half slid, half stumbled down the path, she missed her footing and landed on the rocky hillside with a bump.

'Too much to drink?' she heard Amanda call out.

Liz pulled herself up, embarrassed, and squinted in Amanda's direction. 'Oh, it's you,' she said.

Amanda gave her a watery smile. 'Sorry. I always seem to be popping up at the wrong time.'

'It's all right,' Liz slurred and began to scramble up the hill again, embarrassed.

Back in the pub, Liz drunkenly recounted the meeting in her poshest voice to Karen and Mutley. 'I've just bumped into Amaaaanda Grimsby.'

'Where?' asked Karen, not catching on to the accent at all.

'Dine the hill. I think she thought I was drunk.' Liz took a slurp from her glass and lunged out to grab on to a table to try and steady herself. 'Not that she would know what drunk is,' she continued in her posh accent. 'Probably never touched a drop in her life.'

'Probably has a sherry,' Karen volunteered.

'What, a schooooner of sherry.' And with that Liz promptly sat down on the bench with a thud and started to feel rather dizzy.

Liz was dropped back at the house around midnight by Mutley, drunk for the first time ever. It was the only way she had been able to get through the evening; it had been so depressing and boring and dull, and then she started to feel guilty about being mean about Amanda and felt even worse.

In a daze, she stumbled towards the front door and fumbled around with her keys, not knowing which to use. Everything seemed foggy and vague. She was hardly aware of where she was or what she was doing. And it was so dark, the street lights had been turned off and the moon was obscured by a quilt of thick cloud.

When Liz finally managed to get into the house, she hiccuped loudly and clamped her hand over her mouth. Then, unable to see a thing, she fumbled through the hallway, knocked into the telephone and sent it crashing to the floor.

Suddenly the light went on and Liz saw George standing in the living room doorway. 'Why not make a bit more noise and wake every bleeder up?' he bellowed.

'Sorry, Dad.' Liz's heart began to beat loudly. She was a fly caught in a spider's web and tried to wriggle out by mounting the stairs.

'Where the hell do you think you're going?' George barked. 'Get down here. And sharpish.'

Suddenly another loud hiccup slipped out of Liz's mouth. And then another. And another. And then she felt George roughly grab her arm and drag her off the bottom stair and into the living room. She completely lost her balance on the way and would have fallen over had he not hauled her up with his large, hairy arm. 'No daughter of mine's coming home drunk like some cheap, common slut,' he bellowed. 'Who do you think you are? The cat's bleedin' mother?'

'No . . . ' Liz tried to protest, but another hiccup burst out of her mouth before she could say anything else.

'You're coming with me,' shouted George. He tightened his grip on Liz's arm which was searing with pain and started to drag her out into the hallway and through the kitchen.

Suddenly Liz came to her senses and in a split second she became enraged. 'Let me go!' she shouted, desperately struggling to free her arm. 'You pig. How dare you?'

'Oh, I dare all right. I dare,' George snarled.

'I'll report you for this,' Liz yelled. 'I'll prosecute. I will, I'll prosecute.'

'Just you bloody try.' George fumbled with the back

door and eventually managed to open it, pulling Liz into the backyard. When George reached the coal shed, he opened the door and, with all his strength, hurled his daughter inside like a sack of potatoes. 'That's what happens to anybody who comes home drunk in this house,' he shouted.

'Then you should bloody well move in here,' Liz screamed.

But George had gone. Slammed the door, locked it from the outside and stormed off.

'Great help you were,' said Liz to Sheila the following morning. She was sitting at the kitchen table in her dressing gown and had a towel wrapped around her head in a turban. It had taken her half an hour to get the coal dust off her skin and out of her hair. 'Funny how everybody just disappears in this house when you need them.'

'I was in bed when you came home,' Sheila replied sullenly from the sink.

'You must have heard what was going on.'

'I didn't think he'd go that far.'

'He could have killed me.' Liz picked up the mug of milky tea which Sheila had guiltily put down and took a loud slurp from it. 'He was as pissed as a fart.'

'He said you were.'

Liz didn't answer. She took another noisy swig from her mug and stared blankly ahead.

Sheila finished drying off the few bits of crockery on the draining rack, sighed deeply and turned to face her daughter. She winced as she remembered the look on Liz's face that morning when she had sneaked down to the coal shed and pushed back the rusty iron bolt. Liz was sitting on a heap of coal, leaning against the wall, her arms and legs crossed; she was covered in thick, black coal dust. Sheila wanted to laugh but didn't dare. She just held the door open to allow Liz to make as graceful an exit as possible.

All night, Sheila had lain in bed thinking of Liz down in that coal shed; George was out for the count, lying next to her and snoring like a walrus. She was dying to go down and let Liz out, but she simply didn't dare. If George had woken and found out, all hell would have broken loose. Instead, Sheila had tried to come up with a million reasons why she should not save her daughter, but none of them was very convincing.

'He'd been waiting for you to come home,' Sheila offered timidly in the kitchen. 'It was his last night before going off-shore. You know. He was disappointed.' She leaned against the sink and lit a cigarette. 'You know what he's like if you try and interfere. It makes him worse. Better to let him work things through.'

Liz ignored her. She felt totally alone. Abused by her father and neglected by her mother. She had known for years she couldn't depend on either of them, but now it seemed so clear. It was as though she had known it in her mind, but not in her guts. How many more times did she have to have her head bashed against a brick wall before she would understand? How many more disappointments? How many more let-downs? How much more violence and abuse? If anything, she was angry with herself for expecting anything else. Why should things be different to how they had always been? It was her. She was being weak—again.

'He was disappointed. That's all,' Sheila repeated.

'Oh, shut up. If he killed someone you'd find a way of justifying it,' Liz snapped.

'You know he likes us to be together on his last night.'

'So we can all sit and watch him get pissed.'

'I just think that . . . '

'Just shut up, will you! Shut up!'

'I'm not going to be spoken to like that . . . '

'Why? He speaks to you like that all the time.'

'That's not true.'
'You don't even notice it any more.'
'That's not true either . . . '
'Oh, just leave me alone.'
'I've told you, Liz, I'm simply not . . . '
'Just shut up.'
And then George walked in, looking bleary eyed. His face was sagging and wrinkled and covered in black stubble like a mangy old dog.
As soon as Liz saw him, she glared at him, stood up and walked straight out of the room. George glared back, but didn't say anything.
'I've tried to explain . . . ' Sheila started, going over to the sink to make him a cup of tea.
'Oh, shut up,' George groaned and sat down at the table.

5

George left the house without murmuring a word of what had happened the night before. He gathered Bobby and Sue up in his arms and they relinquished themselves to his embrace like stuffed dummies, unwilling victims, allowing themselves to be kissed, yet hating the feel of their father's rough cheeks and smell of his stale breath. Then George pecked Sheila on the cheek, grunted, 'See you in a couple of weeks, then', and walked down the path towards Muriel Drain and her taxi which were waiting to take him to the heliport. As the car pulled away, George cast a quick look up at Liz's bedroom window; he knew she was there, but she didn't look out. He imagined her, sitting on her bed, twiddling her fingers, waiting for him to go, hating him. He understood her better than she thought. He knew exactly what was going on in her mind and, somewhere, he understood.

The drive to the heliport only took half an hour. The events of the night before kept creeping back into George's mind as the car hummed along the coast road, following a route he had taken so many times in his life, he had lost count years ago. For a second, he wondered why he had reacted so violently to Liz. Was it because he couldn't stand seeing his own daughter drunk? Was he afraid she might follow in his footsteps? George couldn't bear thinking about it and tried to push the whole thing out of his mind again.

When he arrived at the heliport, George jumped out of the car and pulled his bag off the back seat. 'See ya, then,' he mumbled to Muriel who pretended to be offended by his surly ways, though she had never known him behave otherwise.

George walked inside the terminal and looked up at the flight monitor. He scanned the list of flights and when he saw that his was delayed, his face fell. Now, he just wanted to get away from Boughton and distance himself from everything about it. Working off-shore had its drawbacks, but there was no better escape than two weeks of solid fifteen-hour shifts.

George looked around the waiting room; it was thick with cigarette smoke which lingered in the air like cancer. The area was full of men pacing up and down, nervously smoking, or sitting on benches, their arms hanging over their knees as they watched the TV. Others were reading the morning papers, sipping mugs of tea and taking huge mouthfuls of egg and bacon sandwiches. George recognized no one and sat down on a bench next to a thin, nervous-looking boy who was reading a library copy of *Middlemarch*. The boy was no more than nineteen and had thick ginger hair and a pallid white face which was covered in freckles. 'Where are you off to?' George asked, surprising even himself because normally he never struck up conversations. But today he felt like talking. Any distraction would do.

'Blue Gorse,' the boy replied gloomily. George detected a Mancunian accent.

'Me too.'

'The flight's delayed,' the boy said.

'What else is new? Fog probably.'

'I can't see any.'

'We're not stuck seventy miles out in the North Sea. Want a cup of tea?'

The boy nodded miserably. When George returned and handed him the tea, he smiled weakly, displaying a set of crooked, uneven teeth which were short and square like a baby's.

'Been doing this long?' George asked, sitting down and stirring the cup of thick, milky liquid.

'This is my first time.'

'Oh, well, you're a bit green around the gills then.'

'S'pose so,' the boy replied and looked vaguely around him, wondering what on earth he was doing there. It seemed like some weird Kafka-esque dream.

'Got a name?'

'Jimmy.'

'You a steward?'

Jimmy nodded.

'Thought so. Can always tell.'

Jimmy looked up at the flight information monitor. 'Are we going to have to wait long?'

George shrugged his shoulders. 'Who knows? Could be away in half an hour, could have to hang around all day.'

Not comforted, Jimmy sighed, sat back against the bench and closed his eyes. This life wasn't for him. He hated it already. But what were the alternatives? He had settled his future on life as a foreman at the sewing machine factory—until he was made redundant. He'd never expected that to happen. No one had. The factory had been a steady source of employment for the people of Stanbridge for a hundred and thirty-two years.

Afterwards, he couldn't bear to apply for a job; competing with hundreds of others for one miserable, badly paid position. It totally depressed him. He couldn't even be bothered to put a clean shirt on in the morning.

And then one day he had woken up to the reality of the situation: he couldn't look after Michelle and a new-born baby on the dole. So he went straight round to see his brother-in-law who worked on the rigs, along with almost everyone else in his street, and asked to be put in touch with someone who could help.

He had expected good money. When he was told what his weekly wage would be, he couldn't believe it.

George snorted when he heard that. 'Well, you'd better,' he said. 'It's a myth we're all rolling in it.'

'Isn't it true?'

'They know they've got you by the short and curlies. That's why they always recruit from areas where there's no work. They can pick and choose at their whim.'

George looked up and saw his old mate Elvis bursting through the doors, sweat pouring down his bloated red face as he looked around the room in panic.

'Oi! Elvis! Over here,' George shouted.

Elvis let out a sigh of relief when he saw George and strode towards him. 'Thank God. I was sure I'd miss it,' he said in a thick Glaswegian accent. 'The bloody train from Glasgow was delayed and I missed half my connections. Jesus!' Elvis wiped a greasy-looking handkerchief across his brow. 'I'm knackered,' he said and sat down. Then he stood up again, looked around him and sat down again. 'How long's the delay?' he asked, squinting at the flight screen.

George shrugged his shoulder. 'Dunno.'

'Jesus!' Elvis's heart was pounding, his blood thumping through his veins. He strained his eyes to see the monitor. 'Can't see a bloody thing,' he grumbled and then got up and wandered over to take a closer look.

The sight of Elvis terrified Jimmy. He'd dealt with blokes like that before, but always kept his distance because they could never stand him. He irritated them. They always teased him because of his scrawny physique, and even after he had spent three months working out in a gym trying to build up his muscles, he looked much the same. There seemed to be nothing he could do. Elvis, by contrast, was well over six feet tall and had the build of a gorilla with a large beer belly. His mop of dyed black hair was swept back over his head, like that of his eponymous hero, and he had thick sideburns running down each side of his face. On the fingers and thumb of his left hand were tattooed the letters ELVIS, and on the right hand were the letters MUM with whom Elvis still lived on a large council estate on the outskirts of Glasgow.

George sensed Jimmy's fear and vulnerability. Rather than be disgusted by it, he decided to take the boy under his wing as restitution for his behaviour towards Liz the previous night. There was something about this puny-looking waif of a lad which reminded him of Gary; the two had the same sort of look, sinewy and skinny, not a muscle on their bodies as far as George could see. Jimmy didn't look as though he was any more cut out for working on the rigs than Gary was, but at least he was willing to have a go and, as far as George was concerned, that had to be respected. 'You eaten anything this morning?' he asked.

Jimmy shook his head. 'Come on, then. Shirl'll fix you up.'

On the other side of a battered food hatch, Shirl was leaning against the wall, smoking, and aimlessly staring at the thick blanket of flies which had been sucked dry by the 'sizzler' machine. When she sensed George and Jimmy hovering, she snapped out of her trance and rattled off like a robot: 'What can I get you this morning then, ducks? Pie and mash; pie and peas; gammon and chips; egg, gammon, and chips; egg, chips, and peas; pie and chips; or pie, chips, and peas?'

'What's in the pie?' Jimmy asked gingerly.

'Meat.'

Jimmy turned imploringly to George, his face was pale and washed out, his eyes wide open, like a madman's, and filling with tears. He didn't want a pie. He didn't want gammon. He didn't want anything. And, particularly, he didn't want to go to that rig. 'Look, George,' he stammered, 'I think I'll jack it in now. This isn't for me.'

'Don't be so daft,' George said, sinking his hand deep into his pocket and pulling out a wad of money. 'Give him a pie, Shirl, and a double portion of chips. Build him up a bit. He'd fall through the drain if the gaps were a bit wider.'

When their flight was finally called, George levered himself up from the ripped plastic bench, stretched until his hairy belly popped out from under his T-shirt, and nodded in the direction of the check-in desk. 'Come on,' he grunted, 'that's us.'

After they had checked in, both men were frisked as they went through the security point into the departure lounge. 'What are they looking for?' Jimmy hissed after he had watched a guard turn the small canvas bag he was taking on the helicopter inside out.

'Booze. Drugs. Same as what they all look for.'

'I thought no one was allowed to take that sort of stuff off-shore.'

'They're not. But that doesn't stop them trying.'

When everyone was assembled in the departure lounge, a safety video was shown. Most men sat looking around the room, smoking and picking their nails, bored. Jimmy, who was terrified at the very idea of going in a helicopter, sat gulping down every word. 'I could recite that thing off by heart,' George hissed loudly to him when it was half-way through. But Jimmy ignored him; he didn't give a damn if George could recite the Bible, all he wanted to know was what to do if the helicopter suddenly ditched in the sea.

'They do go down, you know,' George hissed into Jimmy's ear during the video. 'The helicopter ride is the most dangerous part of the trip.'

Jimmy remained rigid on his bench and stared ahead of him without blinking.

After the video, everyone clambered into orange survival suits which were like giant romper suits and trooped out to the waiting helicopter.

Once inside the chopper, George handed Jimmy a set of headphones. 'Here, put these on,' he said, 'they'll cut out the noise.' Jimmy took the headphones gratefully, he couldn't bear loud noise, it made him nervous and jumpy.

'Good morning, gentlemen,' the pilot said as he completed his pre-flight check. 'My name's Captain Morgan. First Officer Tom Butley will be flying you out to Blue Gorse this morning. Our flight time will be approximately 50 minutes and we'll be flying at an altitude of 8,000 feet and at a ground speed of around 155 miles an hour. As you've probably noticed, it's a bit blowy this morning, around 40 knots, so please keep your seat belts fastened during the whole trip. Thank you.'

Jimmy strapped himself in and listened, terrified, as the engines were throttled. Then, with a tremendous clatter, the helicopter began to lift slowly off the ground and hover along the airfield to its take-off spot. Jimmy's heart began to pound and his hands grew sweaty and damp. His face was pale and taut as he turned to George who had just poked him in the ribs.

'It's all right really,' said George. 'Only winding you up.'

But Jimmy wasn't comforted. He had heard plenty of stories about helicopter accidents, seen them in the paper. He'd been told pilots could do a controlled landing at sea, but how much control did anyone have if the engine stopped and the blades wouldn't turn? And then, if it landed on the sea, would it float? Or would it sink, taking them with it, trapped in a huge air bubble? The first officer rammed the engine into full throttle and the machine surged forward; it rushed along just a few feet above the ground before leaping into the air and soaring up towards the clouds. Jimmy shut his eyes. There was no going back now. His fists were clenched, his knuckles white, and the palms of his hands drenched in sweat.

After what seemed like an eternity but which was, in fact, just a couple of minutes, Jimmy peered cautiously out of the window. Boughton was already reduced to a toy town and disappeared from view as they crossed the frothy coastline and headed out to sea. A constant stream of helicopters passed them, taking men and supplies to and from the rigs.

Jimmy hated every second of the trip. Some people found it exciting. He found it terrifying. The noise was unbearable. The vibration almost painful, he felt every bone in his body was being shaken loose like a cocktail. And Elvis kept leaning over and cracking jokes, but his thick accent and the clatter of the engines meant Jimmy couldn't hear or understand a word. George didn't bother saying much; seeing how nervous the boy was, he gave a quick thumbs-up sign and grinned once the helicopter had reached its cruising height.

After about half an hour, when they were fifty miles or so out to sea, Jimmy looked down and saw what looked like villages of stick-like platforms in the sea; each rig was standing on stilts and flares burning off excess gas protruded from them. And beside each rig, Jimmy could just about make out a stand-by vessel bobbing around in the sea; these were usually old fishing trawlers which had been roughly converted and were hired by the oil companies to stay within a half mile radius of each rig just in case there was an accident. From the air, the platforms appeared to be connected by broken lines of surf created by the equally dilapidated supply vessels which slowly chugged from rig to rig delivering everything from tinned food to lavatory paper, paint, and spare parts for machines.

As they descended towards Blue Gorse, Jimmy looked down at the rig; all he could see was a massive complex of steel pipes which were interwoven like spaghetti. He whistled through his teeth. 'Where does everyone sleep?' he asked George. 'In pipes?'

'Near enough,' George replied. 'There's an accommodation module somewhere underneath that lot.'

Jimmy could feel the wind buffeting the helicopter as it cautiously lowered itself on to the helideck. 'A chopper fell off this deck once,' Elvis shouted. 'Tumbled straight off the edge. Just like that. Int' the sea.' He made a splatting noise with his lips and turned away, grinning, obviously pleased with himself as he put this new one through his paces.

Jimmy ignored him. He didn't really care what Elvis

thought. Nothing could be worse than what he was feeling: dread, fear, anticipation, terror. The helicopter door was opened and, crouching almost on all fours, the men began to scramble on to the deck which was covered with a thick rope to prevent any more helicopters from slithering into the water. Bending low to avoid the blades which were still spinning above his head like frenzied executioners, Jimmy cautiously made his way across the deck. Suddenly, he lost his footing, slipped and fell. 'For God's sake, you've only just arrived,' George shouted, hauling him up like a child. Almost in tears, Jimmy allowed himself to be picked up like a rag doll. All he wanted was to be at home with Michelle and the baby.

Once inside the iron monster, the men took off their survival suits and hung them on pegs in the waiting room where they would be put on by those returning to shore. They were then taken through the usual safety demonstration and tour of the rig before being allocated their cabins. 'George Dean, you're in No. 15,' said an officious-sounding young steward who was about thirty and had one ear missing. 'Bob Jones, number 19.' The steward went through everyone's name until he finally came to Jimmy's which he read out like an afterthought. 'James Craven, you're . . . you'd better start in number 21 but you'll probably have to move. When you've dumped your bags come back and report to me.'

George showed Jimmy to Cabin 21 and whistled under his breath as he looked inside the newly refurbished room which contained two bunks, a fitted locker for each occupant, and a brand new shower and WC neatly built behind a screen in the corner.

'You won't be staying here long, I'll tell you that for nothing,' George grunted.

'Oh?'

'You'll see.' George gave him a knowing look, picked up his bag and walked down the corridor towards his own, less salubrious quarters. When George arrived at his cabin, the first thing he saw was the bright red, bald head of a man who was bending over his bunk, scrabbling around on the floor. 'What a sight,' said George, dumping his bag on the floor.

The man looked up in surprise. 'George!' he said, his face lighting up. 'Good to see you.' George grinned at his old mate, Andy, and leaned against the wall with his arms folded. 'You look like you're about to explode,' he said.

'Yeah, well, I've lost my bloody lighter.'

George dug a box of matches out of his shirt pocket and threw it across the cabin at Andy. Then he looked around the room; it was much smaller than Jimmy's: four bunk beds were crammed in with four battered lockers which were covered in graffiti and had varnish peeling off; outside in the corridor one WC and shower had to serve every five cabins. 'Who else is in here?' George asked.

'Knockers.'

'Oh God. We'll be awake all night with his snoring.'

'Ask for opposite shifts.'

'That's easier said than done.' George picked up his bag, lugged it over to the row of lockers and started unpacking his things. 'How long's Knockers here for?' he asked.

'Till the end of the week.'

'Well, he'll have to sleep up top. You wouldn't get a wink with him under you.'

'You can tell him.'

'He can think what he wants.'

Once George had unpacked his things, he made his way through the sterile labyrinthian corridors of the accommodation module; each looked the same, each was painted white with the same safety notices and directions plastered over the walls and doorways. He walked to the locker room which was where the men changed out of their work clothes and into their everyday gear; men were not allowed into the accommodation modules in their overalls to preserve, as much as possible, the informal 'homely' atmosphere of this part of the platform. As usual the locker room looked like a tornado had swept through it; cigarette butts carpeted the floor, soft drink cans had been crushed and dropped on the spot, newspapers, magazines, and clothes were strewn everywhere and the walls were papered with pin-ups of naked women which were covered in lewd scribbles. George climbed into a set of red overalls, pulled on his thick leather boots and plonked a hard hat on his head. This was statutory clothing, many were obliged to wear protective gloves and eye masks too.

Even though it was September and not cold, George blew into his hands out of habit when he walked on to the main spider deck. He looked around to see who was there. Up to ninety men worked at any one time on Blue Gorse 365 days a year; at least sixty of them were 'contract workers' meaning they were usually manual workers hired to work on specific jobs for certain periods of time. There were also skilled workers like George who were on longer term contracts. And there were the company men who were actually employed by the company and very much 'masters of the ship'—although they vehemently denied it.

George found himself surrounded by activity; men were hammering and welding, shouting orders from one deck to another, straddled under complicated pipework and struggling with spanners to free nuts and fittings which had rusted and seized up. Because the rig was so exposed to the thick salty water and biting wind, everything rusted and corroded five times as fast as it would anywhere else. In fact the main jacket of the rig had passed its sell-by date some time ago and constantly groaned and strained under the relentless vibrations of the massive drill which bored deeper and deeper into the sea bed. Men worked around the clock, often up to seventeen hours a day; there was nothing else to do.

The rig required constant attention; like a vast, living animal it needed to be nourished and fed, it never stopped breathing and never went to sleep. The gruelling production schedule was only eased for one month in the summer when the system was slowed down for a massive annual overhaul.

As George wandered across the deck, men called out to him and waved; he was a popular figure, liked for his fairness of spirit. He always said what he felt, people knew where they were with George Dean—and that had to stand for something.

Watching the crane operation was Amanda Grimsby's father, Peter, who was the Offshore Installation Manager (OIM). He was in charge of the rig and had similar responsibilities to those of a captain of a ship.

George walked over to Grimsby, his hands sunk deep into his overall pockets.

'You back already?' Grimsby asked, grinning. 'Can't keep you away from the place.'

'You never leave,' George retorted. He didn't like Grimsby. But they had worked together for years, on and off, and had learnt how to tolerate each other.

All morning the sky had been clogged by thick cumulus clouds. Suddenly the sun popped out from behind them and Grimsby put his hand up to shade his small, ferrety eyes. He looked at George intensely for a moment. The last time he had seen him was just after Jim Drew's accident and it brought the memory flooding back. It was a grim business. Always reflected badly on him and it didn't look good for the company either. Now Grimsby was keeping a close eye on the crane operation to ensure there was no repeat performance. 'Jerry's welding up on the starboard ledge,' he said to George, nodding to where huge crates were being lifted out of a supply vessel and stacked on the spider deck. George looked at where he was pointing and his blood ran cold: Jerry, his apprentice, was welding right underneath the unloading operation.

'But they're unloading right over his head!' he shouted almost choking.

'Got to. The supply vessel hasn't been able to get in for two days and we're running out of food.'

'After what happened to Jim Drew!'

'Everything's under control. What do you think I'm standing here for.'

'So take Jerry off the job until the unloading's finished.'

'Can't afford to. Those pipes need to be done now.'

George felt the blood pounding through his body as if it was about to boil over. The image of Jim Drew being battered to death flooded through his mind.

Grimsby looked at George, challenging him, almost smirking. They both knew there was nothing George could say, he was completely powerless. Men who complained too often suddenly found themselves NRBed (Not Required Back) which meant they were blacklisted by contracting companies. The word passed around the industry quickly enough; other companies soon found out that so-and-so was a trouble-maker and wouldn't take him on. They could pick and choose, there was no shortage of men. Grimsby was also perfectly aware that George's two-year contract would end in a couple of month's time and that there was no guarantee that it would be renewed. Even more cause for George to be on his best behaviour. They had him by the short and curlies and he knew it.

This wasn't the first time George had pointed out safety hazards and been ignored. When he first arrived on Blue Gorse he had been horrified by the condition of the pipework and state of the welds; there were cracks and faults everywhere, welds welded welds which welded welds. He reported them, but so many needed to be replaced they'd have to shut the platform down for months, and that meant stopping production which was unthinkable. George had pointed these faults out to Grimsby several times, but he knew when to stop.

He also knew that with over three million cubic feet of highly pressurized gas charging through the rig, everyone working on that platform was sitting on a time bomb. In short, Blue Gorse was an accident waiting to happen.

6

George worked until eleven o'clock that night. He and Jerry, his young apprentice, were checking various welds and pipes on the cellar deck which was the lowest working level of the platform. Many of these pipes should have been replaced, but there was no chance of that happening until the rig went into 'shut-down' mode the next summer when the main bulk of repair and maintenance work was carried out. George always felt gloomy patching up old welds; he took great pride in his work and said it made him feel like a doctor who had to stick bits of plaster over a leg which needed amputating.

When George and Jerry finished their shift, they were replaced by two other welders who would work through the night. Often, when they were working on complicated welds, they had to carry on until the job was finished. There was always plenty to be done on the cellar deck because it was so close to the sea; the pipework corroded even faster than on other levels and always needed attention. 'It's like painting the Forth Bridge,' George grumbled. 'It never bloody ends.'

At the end of the shift, George slowly made his way up towards the main accommodation module. There was less activity on the rig than during the day, but still machinery continued to turn and he could hear the low voices of men working and hammering on the other decks. Normally, he liked working at night. There was something peaceful and soothing about it; there were fewer people around and he felt safe, enveloped by the night, left to drift in his own thoughts. But on this night he was exhausted and still hung-over from the night before. He was tired after getting up so early to leave Boughton that morning and then working a ten-hour shift. His head was throbbing. All he wanted to do was to go to bed, but he knew Knockers would be in the cabin, snoring.

Rather than follow Jerry to the galley for supper, George wandered over to the edge of the deck, leant over the railings and looked out to the dark, black sea. Even though it was late at night, the rig was still humming. It never stopped. It was a hyperactive creature that never went to sleep. Millions of cubic feet of gas burst through its veins, keeping it alive, gushing through hundreds of pulse points in the system before being dispatched to shore. Nowadays, George hardly registered the background noise of the machinery, neither did he notice the vibrations of the drill as it bore deeper and deeper into the sea bed. Like all the other men working out there, George was used to the noise. If anything, it wasn't until he went on shore that he noticed anything: the silence was almost unbearable.

George waited for his eyesight to adjust to the darkness. It felt as though a storm was on its way: the wind was building up and nagged at his hair, and the waves had grown noticeably higher than they were when he had started his shift ten hours ago. He leant over the railings and looked down to where the sea was hurling itself against the rig below, seething white froth swirled around and around the rusty girders in a frenzy. Ahead was nothing but darkness; down was nothing but the hungry, voracious sea. It was a strange sensation, being out there, stranded, miles away from anywhere. He couldn't see the horizon at all. Couldn't make out where the sea stopped and the sky began. Sometimes, when he looked into the blackness of it all, he thought that's what it must be like when you're dead. Just black. Nothing. Nothing out there. Nothing inside.

George fixed his stare on the shadowy silhouette of a

small stand-by vessel which was bobbing around about five hundred yards away. He could just see its lights flickering from the portholes and wondered how the men aboard managed to live for weeks on end crammed together in the makeshift living quarters of an old fishing trawler. What was there to do? Play cards? Read newspapers? Listen to some crackly old radio? Most boats didn't even have a television. And they were totally dependent on the rigs for second-hand newspapers. Those men were really cut off from the world; it was a wonder they didn't all go mad. George thought it must be the worst job in the world.

Suddenly he felt a hand on his shoulder and turned around, alarmed.

'You're a bit jumpy tonight, George,' said Andy. 'Anything wrong?'

'No.'

'First night blues?'

'Maybe.'

The two men were quiet for a few moments and then Andy yawned and stretched his arms out behind him. 'Looks like there's going to be a storm. It's getting a bit nippy out here. Aren't you cold?'

George shook his head and leaning over the railings again looked back down at the sea. He was only too aware of its power. He'd seen it swallow men up in seconds; huge macho scaffolders who had fallen off the side of the rig because they refused to wear harnesses. He had even seen it gobble up a young steward who had thrown himself overboard one night in a fit of suicidal despair. 'Ever wonder where the bloody hell you do belong?' George said quietly.

'It *is* first night blues,' Andy replied.

'Do you?'

Andy moved next to George and leant over the railings too, his arms outstretched, his hands locked together. He took a deep breath and sighed, pushing a long strand of sandy hair back over the bald patch on his head. 'Never used to,' he said. 'But after Linda left me . . . well . . . I don't really feel I belong anywhere now.'

George looked at Andy who seemed subdued and sad. 'At least I've still got the wife,' he said.

'Be grateful for small mercies.'

'She doesn't care. To be honest, I don't think they need me at all.'

'Probably don't.'

George turned to Andy, shocked.

'Come on, George. You've worked off-shore for years. They've learnt to cope without you. They've got their own lives.'

'What about me? What about my life?'

'That's up to you. They can't live it for you. In a way, your life's here. With this bunch of blokes.'

George turned and scowled at Andy. 'That's cheered me up no end.'

'You wouldn't find friends like this on-shore, George. No one understands what goes on out here better than us.'

George was quiet for a moment and then added gloomily, 'Can't talk to Sheila about anything. Couldn't even tell her about Jim.'

'No one makes you come out here, Georgy boy. It's your choice.'

'I'd like to see how they'd keep clothed and fed if I didn't.'

Andy turned to George and raised his eyebrows questioningly. George knew as well as any man that working off-shore had its advantages; if the going got tough at home, it did provide a convenient way out.

Liz had been sitting in the Sea Shell for over half an hour listening to Karen, Heather, and Stacy wittering on about nothing.

'When I asked him what he'd been up to, you know, in a friendly sort of way, he said, "Nothing. I've been depressed."' Heather made a long face and stuck out her bottom lip.

'Oh God!'

'I wouldn't go out with him, Heather. He's bad bloody news.'

Heather turned the sugar shaker upside down and began to trace a pattern in the pile of sticky granules with her finger. 'I know,' she mumbled. 'But I like him. I can't help it.'

'Plenty of others around.'

'Where?'

'I'd bloody well like to meet them.' Karen carefully skimmed the skin off her coffee with a spoon.

'So what about Snot? Are you going to go out with him or not, Liz?'

'No, I bloody well am not,' Liz replied. She was sitting slouched against the wall, her legs stretched out under the table. She was still sulking from the night before when George had locked her in the coal shed. It made her even more determined to leave home, to get out of Boughton, get away from these people, people she had nothing in common with, didn't even want to be with.

'So what are you going to do, then?'

'Leave,' Liz replied irritably.

Heather and Karen looked at each other and raised their eyebrows. 'Not good enough for you now?' said Heather who had always been jealous of Liz and could never resist an opportunity to have a go at her.

'I didn't say that,' said Liz.

'Got someone else, then?'

'No. I am capable of surviving without a bloke, you know.'

Karen, Stacy, and Heather looked at each other in turn, rolling their eyes until they nearly fell out of their heads. Heather had to bite her lip to stop herself from laughing.

'You haven't turned the other way, have you?' Stacy said provocatively.

‘So what if I had?’ said Liz. She’d had enough of this conversation and roughly pushed her way out of the bench seat past Heather. ‘It’s all you lot bloody think of.’

Outside, a fine mist hung over the sea and lingered across the beach like muslin. It was drizzling with rain very slightly and the temperature had dropped for what seemed like the first time in months. Summer was finally gasping its last breath and slipping away quietly. The seasons were on the change. Apart from a few ragged dogs and their owners, the beach was deserted. Most of the caravans had been hooked to the backs of cars and tugged home to be left in front gardens and driveways for another year. The sea was rougher than Liz had seen it for weeks; waves crashed to the shore, smashing on to the shingle, sweeping up the beach and leaving white foamy lather around the breakwaters; she had never seen it so polluted.

Liz zipped up her leather jacket, sunk her hands into the pockets and started to trudge across the shiny wet shingle. Suddenly she heard someone call her name and when she looked up she saw Amanda standing on the promenade in her school uniform carrying an expensive-looking brief-case.

‘Liz!’ Amanda called again and jumped off the promenade on to the beach.

Liz stopped and squinted as Amanda crunched across the shingle towards her. It was odd that they kept bumping into each other, they had barely spoken at school, even though they were in the same class. Somehow, everything seemed to be different now. Liz’s whole frame of reference was changing.

‘Thought it was you,’ said Amanda. She grinned shyly and looked around. ‘Looks like there might be a bit of a storm.’

‘Well . . . yes,’ Liz mumbled.

Amanda lifted up her case. ‘Back to school,’ she said.

'How is it?'

'Oh, the same, you know. Nothing ever changes. Although I don't know if I can stick it for another two years.'

'Really?'

Amanda nodded her head and turned away from Liz. She was biting her lip and her face suddenly seemed creased with anxiety. She sniffed loudly.

Liz stood watching her. She wasn't sure if she was crying or had a cold. She couldn't imagine Amanda Grimsby crying about anything, she always seemed so cool and composed. But something had changed in her. She looked different. Older.

Amanda's blonde hair was not neatly tied back as it usually was, but flying all over the place in the wind. She turned back and looked at Liz, trying to speak. 'I . . . I . . .' she started.

'What?'

'Nothing. Are you religious?' Amanda sniffed again, trying to pull herself together.

'No.' Liz started to walk slowly across the shingle. Then she turned to Amanda, laughing, and said, 'You used to be. I remember. You were the only girl in our class who was confirmed, apart from Jenny Murphy, and she was a Catholic.'

'Oh, God.' Amanda grinned.

'And you were the only person who used to pray in assembly.'

'And you used to tie my shoe laces to the desk so I couldn't file out.'

Liz smiled and turned to look at the sea. The mist was growing thicker and thicker, making it almost impossible to see anything.

'Is your father out there at the moment?' Amanda asked.

'Somewhere.'

'You know he's on the same rig as my father?'

'No.'

'Well, he is. They're on Blue Gorse.'

'Oh.' Liz bent down, picked up a stone and hurled it into the sea.

'Didn't you know?'

'No . . . I . . . '

'What if something happened?'

Liz shrugged her shoulders and picked up another stone. 'Nothing ever does.'

'My mother and I went out last Christmas when Dad was on duty. They flew everyone's family out.'

'We didn't go,' said Liz. 'But that's because your dad's a company man, isn't it?' she laughed and gave Amanda a nudge. But Amanda didn't say anything.

'Come on.' Liz turned away from the sea and, followed by Amanda, started to walk towards the promenade where colourless wooden beach huts lurked like murky ghosts in the mist. She had seen three shadowy figures standing in front of the huts and as she reached the top of the beach she recognized them as Karen, Heather, and Stacy who were standing scowling at her. Liz looked at them coldly and, without a word, walked straight past them.

'Snotty cow!' she heard someone shout after her.

Liz stuck two fingers up behind her back and walked on.

Sarah Grimsby had never got used to being alone, even after all the years her husband had worked off-shore. In fact, her very reason for marrying was so as not to be alone. She hated it. She needed to be looked after. When Peter took the Starco job and began to disappear for two weeks out of four, she felt totally let down. Cheated.

About a week after Peter had gone back to Blue Gorse, Mrs Grimsby had the fright of her life. That night the dirty phone caller had been pestering her again, and then, later, during the early hours of the morning, she was woken by the frenzied barking of Cuthbert, their huge Irish terrier. Her heart pounding, she slid out of bed, slipped on her dressing gown and pulled out the shotgun from under the bed. Cautiously she crept on to the landing and down the stairs; just holding that gun terrified her, she could never use it, she didn't know how to. She had always hoped that just pointing it at someone would scare them away. Meanwhile Cuthbert was going mad downstairs, barking and yelping, hurling himself around in wild circles and trying to jump up against the back door. As Mrs Grimsby groped along the landing, all sorts of scenarios flashed through her mind: Had the dirty telephone caller come to get her at last? Was he a knife-man? An axe-man? What about Amanda? What would happen to her? She might be dead already. What if he managed to take the gun away from her and shot her with it. What if . . . What if . . .

When the police arrived, Mrs Grimsby was sitting in the living room still shaking and drinking a cup of camomile tea prepared by Amanda. 'I'm sorry,' she mumbled to the police officer, 'I wasn't to know. It could have been anyone.'

'You didn't need *all* the emergency services,' said the policeman who was looking very stern as he scribbled in his notebook.

'No one told me the Brownies were camping next door.' Mrs Grimsby took a noisy sip from her cup. 'I thought they had latrines. Holes in the ground or something. They'd scare anyone half to death creeping around the school in the middle of the night. One of them could have got shot.'

'Have you got a licence for that thing, madam?' asked another police officer picking up the gun and examining it.

Mrs Grimsby looked at him blankly. 'I've no idea,' she said. 'It was my father's. And he's dead.'

After George had left, it didn't take long for things to get back to normal in the Dean household. Unlike Sarah Grimsby, Sheila was used to George coming and going and usually breathed a sigh of relief when the taxi pulled away from the house to take him to the heliport. This time was no exception.

As soon as George had left, Sheila went into action. She whizzed around the house removing all traces of him: she took any remaining cans of beer from the fridge and put them back in the cupboard under the stairs, she shoved her husband's shaving gear on the shelves under the bathroom sink which she had built expressly for that purpose, she changed the sheets on their bed and moved the car mirrors back into the positions that suited her. No one would think a man had been anywhere near the house for years.

George's presence turned the house into a prison in which no one could move, or speak, or laugh in case it irritated him. Everyone tiptoed around on eggshells, like dogs trying to please their master. They were so desperate to do and say the right thing, any reward would do: a pat on the head, a smile, an encouraging word. Normally, after George had left, Bobby and Sue charged around like mad things, releasing days of pent-up energy. But this time, Sue stayed calm and controlled and continued to shut herself upstairs in her bedroom with her *Girls Own* annuals and adventure stories. 'Sue's turning into a right little bookworm,' Sheila would say. 'It's not normal. Not for a girl of her age. We haven't seen any of her school friends down here for weeks.'

Even Gary put in the occasional appearance, although he did little more than sit in front of the telly in George's chair. Like his father, he sat glassy eyed, staring at everything and anything that appeared on the screen. Sometimes, he would catch Sheila watching him and would squirm around uncomfortably waiting for her to comment, until she would say gently, 'What the hell are you going to do with yourself, Gary?'

And Gary would fidget nervously and cross his long spindly legs and then uncross them again and say, 'Leave us alone, Mum, will you. Just leave us alone.'

'One day, you'll be chucking old biddies who are younger than you out of the Regal.'

Gary screwed up his face, crossed and uncrossed his legs again, and then got up and lolloped out of the room.

With George out of the way, everyone in the family was beginning to talk about the concert at the Town and Country Club. They were all going: Sheila, Nan and Dad, and even Gary had shown a glimmer of interest. For the first time ever, Liz felt she was going to be the centre of attention and that, at last, she was going to have an opportunity to show her family what she could do. She wanted them to hear her play with other musicians, to watch her perform, to see her in a setting that was totally different to anything they knew, so they could understand that she was accepted by the music world in her own right.

A couple of days later, when Liz was sitting in the kitchen polishing her saxophone and running through the concert for the millionth time in her mind, Sheila appeared wearing a bright blue dress with gold tassels around it. 'What do you think?' she asked, smoothing the material down over her bony body.

Liz looked at the dress and didn't say anything. Finally she mumbled, 'It's all right.'

'You don't like it.'

'I didn't say that.'

'As good as.' Sheila looked at the dress again and smoothed it down over her bony frame. 'Forgot I even had it. Found it rolled up in the bottom of the wardrobe and thought it might be worth salvaging for the big night. You obviously don't think so.'

Liz sat back in her chair and sighed. She had seen her mother return from Norwich the day before laden with bags and knew she had been out to buy a dress for the concert. But because Sheila felt so guilty about buying anything for herself, she always pretended garments materialized out of nowhere and were really no more than old rags. 'It's . . . it's the colour,' Liz offered.

'What's wrong with it?'

'I don't know. It's too bright. Or maybe it's the tassels. Yes, it's the tassels.'

Liz looked at her mother whose face was puckered up as though she were about to cry. Desperate not to hurt her, she stood up and tried to put her arms around her, but Sheila pushed her away. 'No, you're right,' she stammered. 'It looks bloody ridiculous on an old trout like me. I must have gone daft to even think . . . think . . . Oh, I don't know.' And she rushed out of the room, sobbing.

A couple of days later Sheila re-appeared in the same garment. This time she had taken off the tassels and let the hem down so that it fell just above the top of her knee.

'Great,' said Liz, getting up and twirling her mother around the kitchen. 'You look great, Mum.' And Sheila beamed with delight.

So at least the dress was settled.

7

Paul Bradford had been a diver for over ten years. Exploring miles of uncharted underworld hundreds of feet below sea level had been his boyhood dream; as a child he had spent hours swinging in a hammock, meandering along vast underwater prairies and winding in and out of gaping dark coves in his mind. It was the solitude, the quiet, the sense of being so totally alone that appealed to his introverted nature; and it was the excitement of never knowing what could be lying in wait or what might suddenly lunge out from the murky depths that excited the adventurer in him.

After completing his training and spending five years working on oil rigs in the Gulf, Paul had decided it was time to go home. At twenty-eight he felt that he was missing out on life. He had plenty of money, but nothing to spend it on. Still quiet and withdrawn by nature, he bought himself a cottage in the rolling Downs of Sussex and, when he wasn't working off-shore, took up his hobby of watercolour painting again. He then bought himself an old Aston Martin which he spent hours tinkering around with and finally met Belinda, a local girl who ran a craft shop in the next village and with whom he fell madly in love, for the first time in his life.

Life couldn't have been better for Paul. Everything had come together perfectly, like a jigsaw. And although he still felt the same rush of excitement at the beginning of a dive, he no longer cared about earning lots of money; as long as he had enough for the simple pleasures in life, he was happy. Now he just needed to work a few months of the year to keep things ticking over and everything else took care of itself. He wondered why he had never done this before.

That September, Paul went out to Blue Gorse for the first time. There was always a team of divers working on the platform because they had to keep such a close eye on the pipes which ran under the sea, taking the gas back to shore. Paul's job was to change the massive clamps which fix the 'risers', connecting the main import and export pipelines running along the sea bed, to the rig. Like everything else on the platform, the riser clamps became corroded and weakened and needed to be checked and replaced frequently. Cathodic protection helped safeguard the modern underwater fittings, but Blue Gorse had been built before it was introduced and an even closer eye had to be kept on the rig which was almost held together by clamps and welds. The riser clamps Paul had to inspect and change were around thirty metres below sea level; they could be reached using oxygen cylinders, although the divers would not be able to stay down for long and always needed a back-up team.

Before diving, Paul had to familiarize himself with the layout of the platform and the mountain of paperwork required by Starco, the oil company which owned the rig. After he had been given the usual tour of the rig, settled himself into his cabin and grabbed something to eat, he went down to the diving offices and introduced himself to Colin Miller, the diving superintendent.

'Hi there,' said Colin, extending a hand. 'Just hold it a minute, will you.' Colin tapped various instructions into a computer which was sitting on his desk. 'Thought so,' he said. 'According to this you're not meant to be arriving until tomorrow.'

'Oh. Well . . . ' Paul looked at Colin, slightly embarrassed.

Colin put up his hand. 'Doesn't matter. The sooner we

get going the better, as far as I'm concerned. Of course, it does mean more of this.' Colin picked up a wad of papers and plonked it down on the desk again in disgust. 'Take a seat.'

Paul sat down and looked around the small, cramped offices which were crammed from top to bottom with filing cabinets, desks, chairs, piles of papers, maps and charts and diving equipment. He peered through the door and saw a hole in the floor which led down to the dive control and the decompression chambers where divers lived cooped up for days after deep-sea forays.

'Sometimes I feel more like a poxy clerk than a diver,' Colin said. 'There are logs for everything except the Christmas fire, and they've all got to be duplicated a hundred times. If we don't get that bit right they're on to us like a ton of bricks. Bugger the diving. It's the paperwork that counts.'

Paul grinned. He liked Colin's casual, straightforward manner and immediately felt that spending a month on Blue Gorse might not be so bad after all.

Once they left the office, Colin led Paul on to the cellar deck and showed him around the storage areas which contained an Aladdin's cave of diving suits, ropes, tools and special equipment needed for underwater welding, inspection, and diving. They passed rows and rows of oxygen cylinders which sat upright like bombs ready to be fired, before climbing down a small stairwell on to the diving skid which was the platform they dived from. Here Paul saw a mass of winches around which were wound miles of tubing and rope, vital umbilical cords which were attached to divers as they floated around inside the sea's giant womb. A wet bell, used to pull divers in and out of the sea, was also sitting by the side of the platform, together with controls for the air supply and hot water which was fed into the diving suit to keep the diver's body warm as he explored vast, freezing depths. From the diving skid, the two men made their way into the diving control module where they were confronted by a wall completely covered by dials, gauges, monitors, levers, and controls of every description. Paul raised his eyebrows and whistled, impressed. 'You're certainly well-equipped down here,' he said. 'Just as good as the rigs in the Gulf.'

'A lot of it's new,' Colin replied. 'We had a few accidents and finally persuaded Starco to refit the place.'

'Oh?' Paul raised his eyebrows questioningly.

'Sometimes I think the place is jinxed.'

'Doesn't sound very reassuring.'

'I'll tell you over supper,' said Colin. 'Come on, I'll introduce you to some of the blokes.'

It was almost nine o'clock at night and George had had enough. He had been up since six and because he had lost the habit of rising early, felt tired and worn out. 'Come on,' he said to Jerry. 'Let's get some grub before the hordes scoff the lot.' Jerry looked up at George in surprise and lifted the welding mask, revealing a young, sun-tanned face. 'Don't you want to get another pass on this weld?' he asked.

'Let the next shift do it,' said George. 'They'll be here in an hour.'

Jerry looked at George, surprised, and peeled the mask off his head. This was very unusual for George who was always such a perfectionist. They had been welding a pipe with walls almost an inch thick and had to add several layers or 'passes' in order to make the depth. Normally this was work which could not be interrupted, which was why another shift always took over. But for some reason, George didn't think it would matter this time.

'An hour won't make any difference,' said George. 'I'll tell them to heat it up again when they come on.' He began to throw his tools into the big black bag which lay beside him, trying to ignore the fact that his hands were sweating and he had had the shakes all day. He hoped Jerry hadn't noticed that he couldn't hold the iron still; eventually he had handed the job over to him and turned the day into a teaching session. It was the booze, he knew. His concentration had gone, he was irritable and restless, and he could barely restrain himself from snapping at Jerry who diligently worked the weld over and over again, as he had been taught. George knew he was going through some sort of withdrawal symptoms after drinking almost solidly for the past couple of weeks back in Boughton. It happened every time he returned to the rig: he felt awful, swore he'd never touch the stuff again, and then ended up paralytic as soon as he was back on-shore. He felt totally powerless, somehow propelled by a force which took over, which always led him to that first drink, leaving him with no resolve to resist the others which inevitably followed.

George made his way to the locker room and peeled off his overalls as though he were shedding an outer skin. He then put on his own clothes and made his way towards the dining room where men were queuing up and heaping mountains of food on to their plates as they shuffled along in the food queue. Apart from breaks, most of them had been working solidly since seven o'clock that morning and were famished. George wasn't hungry. He felt depressed and tired as though a thick fog had settled inside his brain. He took a tray and waited behind a line of burly scaffolders who were cramming as much food on their plates as they possibly could; soup, meat, potatoes, all the vegetables, gravy, bread, jam roly-poly, custard, biscuits and cheese. They ate like that three times a day; to them it was part of their wages, their due. As far as they were concerned the company squeezed everything it could out of them, so why shouldn't they do the same back?

After George had taken a modest helping of fish, peas, and chips, he looked around the dining room for somewhere to sit. Almost all the tables were occupied by men shovelling food into their bodies as though they may never eat again. The only seats that were free were in an area which was 'reserved' for the company men. Peter Grimsby was there, sitting on his own and reading the *Telegraph*. Sensing he was being watched, he suddenly looked up and saw George standing in the middle of the dining room, staring at him; he raised his hand and jerked his head in salutation and then returned to the newspaper, feeling embarrassed and wondering what was going on. George nodded, blinked and then shook his head to try and snap out of the trance he had fallen into. What the hell was he doing? He couldn't stand Grimsby. In Boughton they virtually ignored each other; Grimsby treated him like some sort of subservient employee, like the gardener or the handyman. Once they had bumped into each other in the Crown and Anchor and he hadn't even bought him a drink. And, of course, George was sure he would have heard about the fight and how he had spent the night in Norwich cooler; that wouldn't go down well on his record, certainly not for a man his age. Lots of the blokes got into fights when they went on-shore, especially after a few jars, but George hadn't done anything like that for years. He was a supervisor, for God's sake, 42 years old. He shook his head and sighed deeply before spotting a place at a table full of noisy riggers.

George ate very little of his dinner. He scraped the remains of it into the bin and then wandered into the lounge where a circle of chairs was arranged around the television which blared monotonously day and night. Stale cigarette smoke and a sense of boredom clung to the air and the walls were covered with yellowing pin-ups of naked women which were about as titillating as flock wallpaper. Jimmy was in the lounge, sitting on one of the chairs with his feet up on the coffee table and smoking nervously. George went and sat down next to him, picked up a magazine and started to leaf through it. 'You finished work already?' he asked.

Jimmy was picking at a dried tomato stain on his trousers. 'Finished a couple of hours ago,' he said.

'All right for some.'

'Head steward said I could go off.'

'What, go and paint the town red?'

Jimmy looked at George, twisted his mouth into a despairing look and then turned back to the television. He wasn't in the mood for conversation. He was fed up, depressed and angry. Already he had been thrown out of his bright new cabin and stuck in what could only be described as a linen cupboard. It had happened that afternoon when he had been sitting on his bed, finishing off the cheese and tomato sandwiches Michelle had packed for him the day before. Suddenly one of the company engineers had appeared at the door. 'Sorry, old chum,' he said. 'This cabin's reserved, I'm afraid.'

'Well, I've only just . . . I thought . . . ' Jimmy stammered.

'Sorry, pal. They should have told you.'

Jimmy looked around helplessly. Sitting there, hunched over that sandwich, made him feel rather stupid. And then a slice of the tomato slid out of the sandwich on to his trousers and dropped on to the floor before he could catch it in time. He began to panic. Suddenly he felt unnerved by this man who was standing there, staring at him in a bemused way. Leaping up, he banged his head on the bunk above, scooped all his belongings out of his locker and backed out of the cabin, virtually bowing and scraping as though the engineer were the queen. 'The chief steward will tell you where to go,' the man shouted down the corridor after him.

Jimmy then found himself in a dark and gloomy linen cupboard without any windows and having to sleep on what was, to all intents and purposes, a shelf. The only advantage of being in this cubby hole was that he did have it all to himself, and that counted for a lot. In fact, as he settled down on his shelf and lay back thinking of Michelle and how this was the first and last time he was going offshore, he began to quite like his new quarters. There was something cosy and homely about them; they were filled with the tepid smell of freshly laundered clothes mixed with the more acrid clinging odour of oil.

'There's too many blokes in here with marriages that bust up,' Jimmy suddenly blurted out to George in the lounge.

'What makes you say that?'

'Because it's true. I was thinking about it. This place is like being in a borstal. Like Alcatraz. No way out. No escape.'

'You like it, then.'

'No, I bloody don't.' Jimmy sat back and lit another cigarette. Stuck out on this rig for two weeks was going to be unbearable. And he had begun to wonder what was going on at home without him to keep an eye on things. To start with, there was the baby, who was getting bigger all the time. And then there was Michelle; Jimmy had started to wonder what she would get up to while he was away. Could he trust her? She'd been around a bit before they got married and she still had that wild streak in her. Who was to say what she might get up to? Jimmy looked at George, wondering if he could talk to him about it, but then he turned away. Things like that were private, he had always been one to keep himself to himself.

The next morning was cold and damp. A dense cloud of mist had descended and wrapped itself around the platform like gauze, and even though the stand-by rescue vessel had moved nearer Blue Gorse, it could not be seen at all. The fittings and machinery were covered with a thin film of dewy water and the air was damp and cold. George was feeling slightly better that day; he was still sweating but shaking less and he had managed to hold the soldering iron that morning without drawing too much attention to his condition, even though he sensed Jerry was suspicious.

When George stepped on to the deck after breakfast, he saw a small group of men muttering and staring downwards. George walked over to see what all the fuss was about: in the middle of the crowd, terrified and confused, was a parrot. It was wandering around in circles, flapping its useless wings and screeching to itself in terror. Its magnificent plumage of reds, blues, and yellows was still radiant in the damp morning air and its beady eyes were roving in all directions as though it were drunk. Every now and again it flapped its wings in a pathetic attempt to fly away, yet it couldn't muster the strength to lift off. 'Don't let it escape,' one of the men called out.

'Someone get some water. Poor bastard must be thirsty as hell.'

Suddenly Elvis pushed his way through the crowd and cautiously bent down a few feet away from the bird. Then he started to make strange cooing noises in his throat and the parrot stopped its manic prancing and looked at him, intrigued. The men instinctively moved back, not wanting to break the spell Elvis had cast. Very slowly Elvis moved towards the bird and then suddenly threw out his huge hairy arm and grabbed it in his fist. The parrot didn't struggle or squeal. With no more than a surprised whimper, it allowed itself to be rescued and then settled into the crook of Elvis's arm as though it had belonged there all along. 'It'll die if we let it go,' Elvis said, standing up and caressing the bird's head. 'It's exhausted already.'

'I say, what have you got there?'

Elvis looked up and saw Peter Grimsby walking over from the accommodation module, his hands in his pockets, a bemused and slimy grin on his face.

No one said a word. For thousand of birds every year, the oil rigs and boats were like stepping stones across the sea. During their great migration south, they touched down when they lost their way in the fog or became exhausted from the journey. After they had landed, some tried to continue their journey whilst others gave up. Either way, the birds rarely survived; smaller species were picked out by the larger hawks and crows, others were poisoned by the stagnant pools of toxic water lying around the rigs, and those which did continue often died of exhaustion. Men used to take the birds inside the accommodation module and try to turn them into pets, but since Grimsby had been OIM he had forbidden it, saying that birds, like all other creatures, had to take their chance with nature and that if the rig was turned into a bird sanctuary it would interfere with the machinery and they'd have droppings all over the place.

That was why everyone held their breath when Grimsby approached Elvis and the parrot. No one knew what he would say or do.

'You know, my daughter has always wanted a parrot,' he finally said.

A sigh of relief.

'Of course, my wife might not be so keen on the idea.'

They tensed up again.

'I'll have to ask her when I call home tonight.'

'It needs feeding first,' Elvis grunted. 'It's starving.'

'OK. Take it inside. But if nothing's to be done with it, it can't stay.'

'I'll keep it myself,' said Elvis.

'Where? It's not staying in the accommodation block for ten days.'

'I'll build it a perch in one of the store rooms. In my own time.'

Grimsby made a grunting noise and moved away. Elvis was furious; he hated that man. Hated him for his lack of compassion, not just for birds but for men too. All the other OIMs used to allow Elvis to put stray racing pigeons in containers and send them back to shore by helicopter where they could be released and returned to their owner under their own steam. Not Grimsby. Again, he insisted they be set free to battle it out with the elements.

George folded his arms and watched Elvis disappear into the accommodation module cradling the parrot. Many a time, he had caught Elvis taking trays of fresh water on to the deck and rushing around the platform, shooing the birds away from the pools of filthy, oily water which lay like greasy plates on the decks. Elvis had even been known to smuggle birds into his cabin and sit there for hours, painstakingly trying to feed them with titbits he had smuggled out of the dining room. Normally, the birds died and he was often seen ceremoniously throwing tiny corpses trussed up in an old vest into the sea, quietly relieved at having been spared the agony of deciding the creature's fate.

Down on the cellar deck Paul was preparing to do his first dive with his diving partner Rick Jones who was otherwise known as Pinocchio because of his unusually long and pointed nose. The two men were lowered into the water in the wet-bell and, once they had reached a few feet underwater, they swam out and began to make their way down to the riser clamps which were fixed to the side of the jacket.

Despite having done this work for so many years, a thrill always passed through Paul's body as he left the wet-bell and began to swim underwater. Attached to him was the 'umbilical' cord which was literally his life-line and kept him in touch with dive control, fed him oxygen, and pumped hot water around his suit. On top of his helmet was a powerful torch which illuminated his path and kept his hands free to work.

When Paul and Pinocchio finally reached the clamp they were to inspect, it became clear that a large crack had formed on the arm fastened around the jacket. The two men looked at each other, raised their eyebrows and then, as the most experienced diver of the two, Paul began to relay details back to dive control.

'How long do you think it'll hold out for?' Colin asked from dive control.

'Not long. It needs to be replaced immediately,' said Paul.

'Shit,' he heard through his ear set. 'Is there anything you can do now?'

'Nothing,' Paul replied. 'It needs a complete replacement.'

'Shit,' they heard again. 'All right. You'd better come up. We'll have to get another team on stand-by.'

When George arrived at the spot where he and Jerry had been working, Jerry was lying underneath a tank examining a series of butt welds they had finished a few months ago. As soon as he heard George approach, Jerry slid out from under the tank and said, 'There's something down here you've got to see, George.'

'Oh God, not another defect,' George groaned, not feeling like tackling any difficulties.

Jerry led George down to the cellar deck and into an area which was a maze of pipes, tanks, and pumps a few yards away from the diving area. Crouching down and making his way through the metal jungle like a monkey, Jerry finally stopped at a large pipe connecting the separator modules which separated the water out from the gas before sending it back to shore. 'My spanner fell down here from the upper deck,' said Jerry, a look of concern on his face. 'Take a look.' Jerry ran his stubby oily finger over a hairline crack they could actually see running around the pipe. It looked deeply embedded in a weld George had done a couple of months ago. 'And smell,' said Jerry, his eyes wide with concern as he watched George's face.

'Jesus,' George muttered under his breath. He could smell the gas five feet away.

'Why haven't the alarms gone off?' Jerry asked.

'Probably seized up.' George looked at Jerry and then swung himself under the pipe to inspect the crack closer. 'The whole pipe needs replacing,' he said. 'I told Grimsby that last year but he wouldn't hear of it because it means shutting part of the system down.'

'Surely it's worth it for that,' Jerry replied.

'Tell him that.'

George straightened up again and stood back to look at the pipe, virtually unaware of the rain which had started to drop on to his hard hat as it dripped down from the girders and pipes above. 'We used a special high-resolution bond last time which I thought might hold until the plant goes into shut-down next summer, but obviously that's no good either. It's the fourth time it's been patched up, you know.' George whistled through his teeth and looked around. 'It just won't hold and that's that,' he said.

'We're not shutting down half of operations just so you can replace one pipe,' said Grimsby. 'We're behind on production already.' He had been rifling through a pile of papers and looking at figures when George arrived. He was worried because head office was putting pressure on him to step up production. George's news was the last thing he wanted to hear. He sat back in his chair and started rocking on its hind legs, obviously angry. 'You'll have to patch it for now, George, and then we'll look at replacing it next year when we shut down for maintenance.'

'You can't patch it any more,' said George. 'It just won't take. The last weld didn't even last two months and it's summer. Winter's coming up.'

Grimsby glared at George through his fierce, ferrety little eyes. He looked as though he might suddenly leap out from behind his desk and fly at him like a Jack Russell. 'You'll just have to find a way of making it hold,' he snarled. 'And if you can't, we'll find someone else who can.'

'We'll have to wait until the weather changes,' George continued, ignoring Grimsby's comments. 'At least until the rain stops and the fog lifts. We don't stand a chance if we can't heat the surface properly. And we'll need ultrasonic equipment to test it.'

'I want it done within the next day. It's too risky leaving it any longer.'

'If the weather doesn't change, there's nothing—'

'Within twenty-four hours,' Grimsby snapped and lifted the telephone. 'I'll have the equipment delivered on the next flight in.'

'And if there's too much fog?'

'That's your problem.'

George scowled at Grimsby and turned to leave. Just as he was going through the door, Grimsby shouted, 'And, George, I want you following full fire precautions when you do this. Make sure you've got fire-fighting equipment on hand and at least two men to man it. And apply for a hot work permit now.' George did not answer, he slammed the office door behind him, furious.

8

When George woke the following morning, rain was splattering against the cabin window and dribbling down in small weepy rivulets. He slowly opened his eyes to accustom himself to the grainy light, then he swung his body out of the bunk, looked at his watch and groaned: it was six a.m. He was too old for this lark. Now, more than ever before, he was beginning to think he'd had enough of working on the rigs; it had worn him down, he didn't know if he was coming or going any more. Still half asleep, George lumbered over to the window and wiped away the condensation caused by a night of heaving and hawking, snorting and farting. Outside, waves up to fifteen feet high rose into the air and crashed against the rig with a mighty explosion. Although the mist had lifted, all George could see was a wildly undulating carpet of grey, murky water which soared and dipped, crashing against itself in anarchic abandon. And from the corner of the window he could just see the stand-by vessel being tossed around like a toy boat. George turned away and wandered back to his bunk. Knockers was still asleep, snoring like a pig and lying with one leg dangling over the side of his top bunk.

'Nothing's going to land here today,' said George gloomily at the breakfast table. In front of him sat a plate of dried scrambled egg which he had hardly touched. All he seemed able to stomach was gallons of black coffee.

'What's the matter with you, George?' said Jerry, belching and sitting back in his chair. 'I've never seen you so miserable.'

George didn't answer. He looked down at the cup and emptied another spoonful of sugar into it.

'And I've never seen you with such a sweet tooth. You must be turning into an old lady.' Jerry let his chair hit the floor with a thump and lurched forward until his face was just a few inches away from George's. 'I reckon it's the time of life, George. You know, mid-life crisis. They say blokes get it too.'

'Don't be so bloody daft.'

Jerry sat back and raised his eyebrows. 'Suit yourself. I look on the bright side. Imagine if we was meant to be going home today and got stuck here for nothing. Think of that.'

'That's always bloody happening.'

'You know your problem, George. You're a right bloody doom monger. All doom and bloody gloom you are.'

When George and Jerry opened the door of the accommodation module and stepped outside they were almost blown off their feet by a ferocious gale whirling across the deck. Battling against the elements, the two men made their way down to the cellar deck and clambered towards the cracked pipe. They could smell the gas five feet away. George felt his stomach lurch with fear; the whole rig could blow at any minute and they'd all be blasted off the face of the earth. They were literally standing on an unexploded bomb. It was a miracle more accidents didn't happen. 'God must look after riggers as well as drunks,' he mumbled as he slid under the pipe to take a closer look.

Five minutes later George was back in Grimsby's office. Once again, he found himself standing to attention like a naughty schoolboy. 'I can't be sure we can heat the weld enough to get a good bond,' he said. 'It's pissing down out there and freezing cold.'

'Leave the jacket on longer,' said Grimsby.

'There's no guarantee that'll do it,' George replied.

'Well, it's got to be done. And I want it started now. It's

too dangerous leaving a pipe like that leaking gas. It could blow the whole lot of us to Kingdom Come.' Visibly angry and growing red in the face, Grimsby stood up and began to shuffle papers irritably from one part of his desk to another, slamming a couple of books on the floor and then dumping a huge pile of paperwork on top of them. 'I've got enough on as it is,' he continued. 'For Christ's sake, George, you should be able to do this sort of thing with your eyes shut.'

George almost felt sorry for Grimsby. 'If the weld's not heated properly and we get an inclusion, the crack will propagate and we'll all be up shit creek,' he said deliberately and quietly.

'I know that. I'm not a bloody idiot.' Grimsby was furiously going through the books on the floor, flinging them into piles and shuffling them around like cards. He stood up and slammed a couple of them on to his desk. 'Just do it, George, will you. Just do it.'

Grimsby stood watching George leave his office, scowling. He'd known there would be trouble when Starco first put him in charge of Blue Gorse; it was so old it should have been relegated to the scrap heap years ago. Of course production was behind, something was always going wrong that required part of the platform to be shut down. Grimsby knew as well as everyone else that the rig was unsafe but, apart from abandoning it completely, they simply had to carry on and hope for the best. Against all odds, it seemed to hold itself together. Yet in his heart, Grimsby knew that it was only a matter of time before something serious happened.

Later that morning, Paul was sitting in dive control looking through various charts and maps which showed where the risers were fixed to the jacket of the rig. He'd already looked over most of the diving kit and, although much of Blue Gorse's technology was bang up to date, their diving equipment was old and in desperate need of replacement. He bit his lip, folded his arms and sat back to watch Colin who was hunched over the keyboard of his computer. 'You look like you're trying to play the "Moonlight" sonata on that thing,' he said.

Colin grinned. 'Couldn't do without it.'

'Where did you learn to use it?'

'Company sent me on a course.'

Paul was quiet for a few moments. Even though he worked in an industry which was so dependent on technology, he didn't like computers at all. He secretly worried that one day they might take over from people altogether and that the world would be run by robots. 'We're going to need another shift to back us up,' he said. 'Pinocchio and I won't finish the job in one dive, especially if there are any complications.'

'I've got that in hand already,' said Colin. 'We've got a back-up team on stand-by.'

'Great. When will we start?'

'When the weather calms down. The forecast says it will clear tomorrow.'

'So we're in for a few rounds of poker today?' Paul said.

Colin nodded at his machine. 'Want me to show you how to use this thing?'

'No thanks.'

The pipe with the faulty weld had to be shut down and isolated and all the gas channelled to the separator through another route. Before the welding could start, the men had to heat the pipe with a jacket made of rods which, in normal conditions, would prepare the surface to create a clean bond. But because the outside temperature had dropped and the rain was pounding down, George was worried that by not getting the weld to a high enough temperature or by not having time to do things properly, an 'inclusion', or foreign particle, would get into the bond and eventually cause it to crack again. If that happened, they'd all be in trouble.

For several hours George and Jerry crouched over the pipe, adding one layer or 'pass' after another. They both wore special masks to protect them from the light of the rod which emitted heat of up to 600 degrees centigrade. Two men stood in attendance with fire-fighting equipment; one with a fire blanket which was spread out on the floor and covered the surrounding pipework, and the other stood like a sentry brandishing a fire extinguisher. Every now and again, the men would stop work to take a breather; during one of these breaks, George saw a small cloud of cigarette smoke being whisked away by the wind near one of the men. 'Are you bloody mad?' he yelled, storming over to him. He ripped the cigarette out of his mouth, stubbed it out on the deck and then kicked it contemptuously over the side. 'If I ever see that again, you'll be off this rig in two seconds flat,' he shouted.

'And I hear you won't be far behind me,' the man sneered, wandering off with his hands in his pockets.

George glared at the man for a second. 'Just bloody watch it,' he said, furious, hurling his fist in the air and walking backwards towards Jerry who was starting to heat the pipe up again.

When life on the rig began to creak into action the next day, the sun was shining and the sky was blue and almost cloudless. The men were in better spirits and, rather than linger over their cups of tea and cigarettes, they wanted to get outside and start work. George wandered down to the cellar deck to inspect the pipe; having worked on it for almost ten hours solid, it had finally been turned on again and appeared to be functioning normally. He ran his rough hand around the smooth weld; it seemed all right, but they'd never know how well it had bonded until they could test it with ultrasonic equipment which would be able to show up the smallest fault or inclusion. The tiniest particle of dust or dirt could have triggered a minute, hairline crack which could expand in hours and result in a catastrophe. But George knew there was no point examining it with the naked eye; worried, he frowned, screwing up his large shaggy black eyebrows, and wandered back to where Jerry was hanging almost upside down inspecting a series of butt welds.

Paul and Pinocchio clambered into their diving gear and prepared themselves to be lowered into the sea in the diving bell. Colin sat at the dive control monitoring everything by keeping a careful eye on the mass of whirling dials and screens in front of him. 'Switch the water pumps to manual,' he commanded down the microphone. This was standard procedure when divers went down because if the fire alarm went off, the water pumps were automatically triggered into action and could suck the divers in with the sea water and literally splatter them over the decks. Colin maintained constant radio contact with the men throughout the dive; he flipped a set of switches in front of him and bent forward to speak into the microphone. 'Prepare to dive,' he said. 'Three, two, one. Go. Dive in process.'

The dive bell containing the two men was lowered into the sea like a great cauldron. As they went down, Paul and Pinocchio could hear Colin's voice crackling through their ear sets: 'Ten . . . fifteen . . . twenty metres . . . twenty-five . . . thirty. You should almost be there now. You've got maps.'

Jimmy was into his sixth day on the rig and beginning to settle in. He still didn't like it, but a couple of the blokes had been quite nice to him and, like a dog grateful for any scrap of human kindness, he lapped it up.

The night before, two men had started to fight over a seat in the lounge.

'You don't own this chair, you know,' growled Popeye when Dave returned from the loo to find his place taken.

'No. But I've been sitting in it all bloody evening.'

'Then it's about time someone else sat in it.' Popeye, so named because of his bulging eyes, calmly put his feet up on the coffee table and picked up a magazine.

'Listen, you little shit . . . ' Dave suddenly turned red in the face, grabbed Popeye by the neck of his jumper and tried to haul him out of the chair. Popeye was on to Dave in a second and they were soon rolling around the floor with four other men, including Elvis, trying to pull them apart.

'For Christ's sake, you two,' Elvis growled, separating them almost single handed. 'Do you want to work or not?' The two men backed off, glaring and snarling at each other like a couple of wild dogs. 'Because if you don't, I know plenty of blokes that do,' Elvis continued.

Jimmy left this scene as soon as it seemed safe to go. He couldn't bear violence, his parents used to scrap and fight all the time and even then he used to go and hide in the cupboard under the stairs.

Jimmy had quite settled into his laundry cupboard; whenever things got too much for him he would disappear into it like a fox diving into a hole. A single light bulb hung from the ceiling and the walls covered in brown hardboard made the room seem even more bare and austere. Yet it provided a safe haven from the threatening, macho world of the riggers and Jimmy relished the idea of installing himself on his shelf and retreating into the neo-Gothic world of *Wuthering Heights* or the cool head of Fanny Price.

Jimmy had always been an avid reader, particularly of the classics: Jane Austen, Thomas Hardy, Charlotte Brontë, Trollope, Dickens—he'd read them all. They provided his great escapes. When he had worked at the factory, everyone teased him because as they flicked through the pages of the *Mirror* or the *Sun*, his nose was well and truly stuck into *Crime and Punishment* or *War and Peace*. At least, being off-shore he had a chance to indulge in his love of reading. At home, there was always the baby, and Michelle didn't like him doing anything that took his attention away from her. 'You don't want to read that old rubbish, do you?' she'd say. And Jimmy smiled sweetly, because of course he did, but he didn't want to upset her either. He hoped that one day she would get used to it. So far, not so good.

That morning a supply vessel had managed to get through. It delivered five quads of oxygen, containing sixty canisters in total, and ten tons of food. Elvis spent the whole morning shifting the supplies down to the store rooms. Before going for lunch, he decided to take a small detour and slithered down a ladder to the cellar deck. It was down here, near the diving deck, that the canisters of oxygen and helium were kept. As much diving as possible was done during the summer months when the weather was good, often with two teams going down at a time. Colin always built up stocks of equipment and supplies because there was nothing more frustrating than running out of the bare necessities. Nearby were several workshops which were used for repairing diving equipment and welding. And then, a bit further along, were a couple of storage huts containing paint and thinner.

Elvis made his way to the first hut, flipped back the catch and walked in. 'Hello, my darling,' he said, a broad grin sweeping across his face. 'What have you been up to, then? Not getting yourself into mischief, I hope.'

The parrot squawked and fluttered its wings in affected irritation and then hopped on top of an iron girder leaning against the wall. Elvis reached up and gently ran his hand over the smooth feathers of the bird, cooing to it all the time. 'Now, I don't want to keep you in here, but it's for your own good, see. I know it's a lovely day out there and all you can probably think of is heading off east, but you'll never make it.' Elvis's eyes filled with tears as he thought of the thousands of birds which dropped into the sea during their migration, dead from exhaustion. 'How any of you ever think you'll get that far beats me,' he continued. 'Now, you've got your water. Let's check your seed as well.'

Elvis glanced over to two saucers which were sitting on a window ledge; one was full of water over which a dusty film had formed and the other contained seed and grain. He could see the bird hadn't touched the food at all and his eyes began to spout tears again at the thought of even this beautiful creature dying. So many birds and animals had passed through his hands over the years, so many gains and so many losses. As a boy, he used to keep birds in his nan's rickety shed at the end of her allotment. His dad kept pigeons too and had converted the top of the house into a loft where he would spend hours fussing around and preening them. But his father never wanted to know about the half-dead sparrows or starlings with broken legs that Elvis brought home. Elvis turned back to the parrot. 'We'll get a good home for you soon enough,' he said reassuringly. 'Don't you worry.'

Peter Grimsby was sitting in his office sifting through more paperwork. He didn't feel like going into the dining room and having to mix with the other men; instead he opted for a light salad which was brought in by one of the stewards. He had to watch his weight these days, he had had a slight heart murmur the previous year and the doctor had told him to go easy on the food, booze, and work. Grimsby was one of Starco's longest serving OIMs and had run Blue Gorse for over five years; even when he wasn't there, he worried about how things were going and phoned in frequently from home for the latest production figures. He was a solid, dependable company employee who lived, ate, and breathed Starco. Having slithered over the other side of fifty, he was now worried about where his future lay; working off-shore was really for younger men, and when you were responsible for that many personnel and that much equipment, you had to have your wits about you. His boss had already started to hint about an office job on the mainland. The very idea of it made Grimsby's blood curdle. He could see himself being put out to salvage like the old boats and disused platforms, broken up for scrap and chucked on the heap.

Grimsby put down the fork and sat back, absent-mindedly examining the remains of the salad sitting in front of him. He then looked at the picture of his wife, Sarah, and daughter, Amanda. It was three years out of date and he reminded himself to change it when he was on shore again. He thought of his home in St Margaret's Drive and how he had finally been able to give his wife what she had always dreamed of: a four-bedroomed, detached house. He thought of Cuthbert, the dog, forever breaking wind at the most inopportune moment, and he thought of his garden and wondered whether the lawn would need mowing when he got back. He looked at his watch, he'd give them a ring in a couple of hours.

Elvis looked at his watch too. If he didn't get down to the galley, there'd be nothing left once those scaffolders had worked their way through the food like vacuum cleaners. He stroked the smooth head of the parrot again, made a few gurgling noises in his throat and left the shed. As he flipped the catch of the door and turned to make his way to the upper levels, he suddenly saw a huge cloud of gas burst into the air from the cluster of pipes he had seen George and Jerry working on. A bolt of panic surged through him and he looked around desperately for cover. But before he could move an inch there was a massive blast which shook the whole rig, sending everything, including Elvis, flying.

The usual background din of chatter and banter and knives scraping across plates was cut dead by the sound of the explosion. As soon as the men heard it, everything went quiet; they looked around, their faces pale, a look of fear in their eyes. George virtually choked on his fish. As though he had been waiting for this to happen, he spat the food out on to his plate, leapt to his feet and shouted, 'Everyone out. Come on. To your muster points. You know the drill. And for God's sake don't panic. And don't push.'

The men needed little encouragement to move. But they were barely out of the dining room when the rig was rocked ferociously by the second explosion; this one happened as the quads of oxygen and helium stored only twenty yards away from the faulty pipe blew. The whole accommodation module rocked and walls began to cave in on themselves; men fell over each other, shouting and pushing, some heading for the storeroom where they knew they would find survival suits, others making their way to the muster points where the lifeboats were waiting. Their cries of alarm were fractured by panic and fear as they realized something serious was happening.

Grimsby leapt off his chair. He had been taking an afternoon nap and the explosion had rocketed him back into reality in a split second. Immediately his heart started to pound and the palms of his hands sweat. This is it, he thought. Jesus, this is it. He rushed out into the corridor to be almost bowled over by men running in the other direction, away from the dining room. 'Go to your muster points,' he shouted out ineffectually. 'To your muster points everyone. And prepare to evacuate.' But his words were drowned by the second explosion and he could see that the endless drills and safety procedures were totally useless. Suddenly all the lights went out and everything was dark. Men started to shout and become disorientated as they groped around blindly. Wide-eyed with fear, Grimsby rushed into the control room and started hammering at the radio shouting, 'Mayday! Mayday! Immediate assistance required!'

An engineer rushed into the control room and started

banging away at the fire pumps. 'Why aren't the bloody pumps on?' he shouted. 'Nothing's happening out there. There's no water.'

'The divers switched them off,' shouted Grimsby. 'Get them on. Now.'

'The divers are still down there.'

'I don't care. Just get the water pumps going.'

Already large black clouds of smoke were buffeting their way along the corridors. Although Grimsby hadn't been outside, he knew a massive fire was raging not far from the main accommodation module. 'What's happened to the emergency lighting?' he yelled at the engineer. 'I thought it was meant to go on.'

'The whole circuit's blown. Look, the high gas warning light's going crazy.'

'Fat lot of good that is. The place is like a bloody tinder box.' Grimsby scanned the controls which were going up and down like ping-pong balls. 'We've just had a ton of paint stripper delivered.'

'Where is it?'

'On the spider deck, starboard side.'

'That's where the explosions were.'

'Oh my God!'

And then there was another explosion. A massive, earth-shattering blast that shook every bone in their bodies. The two men looked at each other. They felt useless and didn't know what to do. 'Come on,' said Grimsby, 'we'd better get the hell out of here.'

The first explosion was only fifty yards from the dive control module and as soon as it happened, Colin Miller immediately started giving instructions to the divers without wanting to alarm them. 'Drop everything and come up immediately,' he ordered. 'Immediately.' He tried to keep his voice calm, but the blast had impacted on the dive module so badly that the walls were cracking and it looked as though they were about to cave in, taking all the equipment with it. Colin looked around him and bent over the microphone again. 'Are you reading me? Come up immediately. Immediately. Drop everything.' He was relieved to hear a crackly voice through his headphones which sounded very far away.

'We're on our way.'

Paul and Pinocchio had almost finished fitting one of the riser clamps and were preparing to return to the surface for air. They both felt the explosion and saw the jacket of the rig shudder violently; it was a few seconds before they heard Colin's instructions over the radio and they could tell something serious had happened by the tone of his voice. Even though they were on a shallow dive, they were still thirty metres down and the umbilicals which supplied them with air were life-lines. If anything happened to the equipment, they would be in deep water, literally. Immediately, they dropped their equipment and started swimming back to the bell; it was then that they felt the second, even greater, explosion of the oxygen cylinders. Then the radio went dead.

The two men looked at each other, worried. Suddenly Paul saw water bubbling in a wild frenzy just twenty metres away and he knew that the water pumps had been turned on. 'Get into the dive bell and hang on,' he shouted to Pinocchio, and then, realizing the radio was dead, started gesticulating madly with his hands. While the pumps were going it was too risky for them to try and swim to the surface because he couldn't be sure they could swim against the pull of the pumps and avoid getting sucked inside. Now, without contact with dive control, they were more or less stuck. The choices were to stay where they were and drown, swim to the surface and get sucked into the water pumps, or hope that Colin in dive control would make a calculated guess that they had reached the diving bell and pull them up. They opted for the third choice, unaware that dive control no longer existed.

9

Liz had almost managed to forget about the concert until she woke that morning. Then, as she turned over in bed and lay staring at the stain on the wallpaper, the imminence of the whole event suddenly hit her and seeped into her stomach like thick cold liquid. That very night was the night. The night that could shape her whole future. Everyone was going to be there. All the family, even old Nan and Dad were going to creak along in their Sunday best. At long last she could play for them, so they would understand, take her seriously, know that she did exist in her own right, outside them. Lying there, as the sunlight streamed into her bedroom, she suddenly felt sad that George would not be there. Even though she felt she hated him, she wanted him to see her up there on that stage more than anyone. He had started her on the road. These were his dreams she was realizing, and he wasn't even going to be there to watch it happen.

Liz decided to work at Roxburgh Hall that morning. She had practised as much as she could and wanted to forget about the concert. Of course she couldn't. As she cycled back from work, her body was seething with a strange mixture of trepidation and fear, rather like when she had taken her school exams, but worse. The sun was out, illuminating an almost clear blue sky. Everything was ready. She had practised and practised and couldn't hope to play 'Stormy Weather' better. Even the band was playing well together. As she breathed in the last of the warm summer air, she threw her fist into the air and laughed. She *knew* that night would be a success. She *knew* it was the beginning of a new life for her. She *knew* it was her ticket out of Boughton. Everything seemed so perfect. It was what she had always wanted.

When Liz got home, she was immediately hit by an air of disaster. Everyone was sitting in the living room: Gary, the twins who were both in tears, and Sheila who was also sobbing and still wearing her oily overalls and clasping a chisel. The television was on and they were all huddled around it in a circle. Liz's high spirits crashed down to earth and her elation switched to fear and panic in a split second. Her hands began to shake. 'What's going on?' she asked.

Sheila was crunched up on the chair like an old car crushed into a cube for scrap. Her face was stained by tears and when she saw Liz she started to cry again. Her lips were stretched taut over her mouth and she was unable to speak for a few seconds. Finally she blurted out, 'There's been an accident. It's your dad.'

'What happened?' Liz looked around the room, she could feel her level of panic and confusion rising like a thermometer in a heat wave. Bobby and Sue were sitting on the floor, leaning against Sheila's legs, pouting and weeping, and even Gary looked upset as he sat on the sofa, his stare fixed to the television. No one said anything and Liz looked around again. 'What the bloody hell's happened?' she shouted.

Sheila looked up, her eyes were like peepholes, vacuous and red around the rims. 'There's been an accident,' she said again.

'I know that. What sort of an accident?'

'On Blue Gorse. Where your dad's been working.'

'What's happened.'

'I don't know. An explosion. Something like that.'

'How do you know he's on it?'

'Because he's been there for almost two years. Look.' Sheila pointed at the television which was broadcasting pictures of Blue Gorse totally immersed in flames, a massive cloud of thick black smoke spiralling into the air. The rig itself seemed to have disappeared into the inferno and looked fragile and rickety, as though its knees were about to break and it would crumble into the sea like Meccano. Liz felt shaken through and through. She couldn't believe it. Shocked, she slowly sat down next to Gary and, with her mouth half open in disbelief, watched the television screen. 'Oh my God,' she mumbled as she watched the rig break up before her very eyes. She looked at Sheila for reassurance, but her mother was too absorbed in her own grief. 'When did it happen?' she asked.

'About an hour ago,' said Sheila, barely noticing Bobby who, snivelling away, had crawled into her lap like a cat and sat there with his thumb in his mouth.

'Nan heard it on the news,' Gary chipped in. 'Then she got Dad to go round to the Regal and ring us. Otherwise we wouldn't know ourselves.'

'I've been telling them to get a phone for years,' Sheila snapped. 'I knew something like this would happen.'

'Jesus.' Liz sat back and stared at Gary for a moment. She had never seen him so animated. She was tempted to make a sarcastic comment and then stopped herself, it didn't seem the right moment. She diverted her attention back to the television again: surrounding the rigs was a massive flotilla of boats of all shapes and sizes which were desperately trying to spray water on to the inferno. Helicopters buzzed around the skies like insects attracted to the heat, dipping and diving, seeing how near they could get, and then making a hasty retreat.

'I knew something like this would happen one day,' said Sheila, snivelling into a soggy tissue which had all but disintegrated in her sweaty clenched fist. 'I always told him not to be so daft and to get an ordinary job like everyone else.'

'That's a lie,' spluttered Gary. 'You couldn't wait to get him out of the way.'

'What do you mean?' Sheila looked over at her son, more amazed that he had spoken than by what he had said.

'You never wanted him around.'

'That's a shame-faced, bloody lie.'

'No, it in't. And you know it.' Gary sat back in the sofa, pursed his thin lips together defiantly and turned back to the television.

'We're going to have words after all this is over,' Sheila stammered. And then she started to cry again, her bottom lip trembling as she added, 'If it ever is over.' And off she went again.

'Sssssh,' said Sue suddenly chipping in. 'They're saying something.'

Everyone looked back at the screen; a young reporter was standing on the sea front of Boughton and in the background they could see the processing plant and the sea.

'Look, Mum, it's up the road. It's Boughton—' Bobby suddenly squealed in excitement.

'Sssssh.'

'It is. Look.'

The commentator started: 'No one knows what caused the first explosion or the extent of the casualties, but what is certain is that this is the end of the Blue Gorse production platform. All radio links with it were lost shortly after the second explosion and because of the tremendous heat emitted by the fire and the vast amounts of burning gas released into the atmosphere, it's virtually impossible for rescue vessels and helicopters to get near enough either to extinguish the fire or to take men off. Roger Bond is aboard a Boughton Rescue Service chopper. Roger, what's going on out there?'

The picture switched to Roger Bond who was fully kitted out in a survival suit and crammed into a passenger seat behind the two pilots. Behind him, through the front screen of the helicopter, it was possible to see the inferno. 'Well, I've never seen anything like it, David,' he started.

'It's now well over an hour since the first explosion, and the sky and the sea are thick with black smoke and flames. It's impossible to get near the conflagration because of the searing heat, but men are being picked out of the water by life rafts and rescue boats.'

'Any idea how many survivors have been found so far?' David asked.

'No. But there were eighty-eight men on the platform and judging by the scale of the disaster it's pretty obvious that casualties will be high. As you can see, there's a thick cloud of smoke mushrooming into the sky and millions of cubic feet of pressurized gas are on fire. I'd say this is the worst disaster to ever hit the North Sea.'

At this point Sheila let out a long moan and grabbed Bobby closer to her so she could sob into his shoulder.

'Do we have any indication of what might have started the fire?'

'My guess is it'll be some time before we know. But what I do know is that on top of the vast quantities of gas passing through these rigs, they are also loaded to the gills with almost every inflammable material you can think of.'

'Such as?'

'Well . . . paint, paint stripper, diesel, machinery oil. You name it. It wouldn't take much to set that lot off.'

The presenter signed off and the screen switched back to a cookery programme with the promise of further news as and when it happened. A helpline number for any concerned relatives was then flashed on the screen every few minutes. 'Have you tried that number?' Liz asked immediately.

'Haven't stopped. Go and try it again, Gary.'

Gary pulled himself off the sofa and lolloped out to the telephone. Liz just sat there, staring blankly ahead, feeling empty and vacuous. She had stopped shaking and suddenly began to feel strangely calm, as though none of this was really happening at all. She looked around the room at her mother, her younger brother and sister, watched them crying, tearful, devastated, and yet she didn't feel anything at all. She felt numb.

A short while later, Nan, Dad, and Arthur arrived. Muriel had driven them over, without charging, considering the circumstances, and, of course, because she wanted a part in the drama too, however small it might be. Muriel took it upon herself to help Dad into the house, even though he insisted he could walk perfectly well. 'It's the shock of it,' she said. 'You can never be too sure of the effect it might have. His legs might cave in altogether.' Once the two old people were installed on the sofa, still wearing their coats, Muriel said, 'I think you could all do with a nice cup of tea.' And she went into the kitchen and busied herself with the kettle and tea bags, while Arthur, who was still dressed in his oily overalls and hob-nailed boots, stretched out on the floor and started to stuff a filthy old pipe with tobacco.

'I'll never forgive myself,' Nan finally mumbled, after they had been sitting there a good few minutes in silence. 'Never.'

'For what?' Sheila snapped. She wasn't exactly thrilled to see Nan and Dad arrive, but decided to ignore them. She had barely noticed that Muriel had edged her way on to the scene.

'Never,' said Nan, ignoring the question.

'Go and try the emergency number again,' Sheila instructed Gary.

'They said they'd ring when they had news.'

'Well, you try them. You never know.'

'But . . . '

'Just try it, will you. And make sure they've got the right number for us. And don't stay on the line too long in case someone is trying to get through.'

Gary sniffed loudly and left the room again. The atmosphere was stiff and tense and it made Liz nervous. She had moved to the floor to make room on the old brown sofa for Nan and Dad and as she looked around at the long, dismal faces she suddenly wanted to laugh.

'If he is gone, I don't expect to see many tears shed in this house,' Nan suddenly blurted out, wiping the corners of her aged eyes with a pink embroidered handkerchief. Then she blew her nose violently and woke up Dad who had fallen asleep already. He looked around the room wondering where he was and then got embarrassed for dropping off at such a moment.

The atmosphere tensed. Sheila jutted out her jaw, pursed her lips together tightly and turned to her mother-in-law. 'What's that supposed to mean?' she snapped.

'What I said,' Nan replied defiantly, without looking at Sheila.

'Well, I think you'd better explain.'

'Come on, you two. Let's get a cup of tea down y',' said Dad, anticipating trouble and trying to haul himself out of the sofa without success.

'No. I want to know what Nan meant by that comment,' said Sheila. 'She can bloody well explain it or take it back.'

'When he is home, he's a stranger in his own house,' said Nan, still staring straight ahead. 'You never want him around.'

'That's a lie.'

'It in't. And you know it perfectly well. He spends all his time at ours or down the boozer.'

'Only if he's got nothing else to do.'

'Doesn't even feel comfortable in his own home. Well . . .' Nan started to try and rub a stain off her pinny which she was still wearing. 'I told him right from the start he was on to a loser.'

'Oh, well, thanks a bloody million.'

'Don't like to say it.'

'Yes, you do. You bloody do. You're jealous, that's all. If you had your way you'd have him still living at home like Arthur.'

'At least they get looked after.'

'Looked after! They're men not babies!'

'Oh, just shut it, the both of y',' Arthur snapped from the floor.

'You're as bad. Worse! Still living at home at your age. It's a bloody disgrace.' Sheila nervously picked her cigarettes up and planted one in her mouth. She was furious and could feel the veins in her neck throbbing like pumps.

Nan had started crying again and allowed Dad to rest a comforting hand on her knee. 'I never thought we'd see him go before us,' she wailed softly. Dad pursed his lips together and stared at the screen; he wasn't quite sure what was going on, it all seemed a bit like a dream really.

'All right, all right,' said Arthur. 'Now, no one knows what's happened yet, so just stop it. Muriel's made us all a nice cup of tea, so let's put the Third World War on hold for the time being, shall we?' Muriel walked in with a tray laden with cups, saucers, milk, and the big brown tea pot. Once she had poured everyone a cup, she poured one for herself and sat down, determined to sit this one out to the end.

Liz couldn't stand the atmosphere any longer. She got up, left the room and went outside to fetch her bike. Suddenly she had remembered Amanda and her mother; she envisaged the two of them sitting, surrounded by all their finery and fancy gadgets, alone. Without thinking, she leapt on to her bike and pedalled off to St Margaret's Drive.

Amanda answered the door and smiled milkily at Liz as though she had been expecting her. Words seemed superfluous and Liz followed Amanda into the large open sitting room which had french windows leading on to a patio and a smooth green lawn. Sarah Grimsby was lying on the sofa wearing a pair of dark glasses and a scarf around her head, looking like Jackie Onassis. As soon as she saw Liz, she took the glasses off. 'Who are you?' she asked, her voice crackling with disappointment.

'It's Liz, Mum. She's a friend from school.'

'This is hardly the time.' Mrs Grimsby magically produced a large gin and tonic which she had been hiding behind the sofa and took a swig.

'Her father's on Blue Gorse too.'

'Oh.' Mrs Grimsby looked Liz up and down and then said, 'I thought you were from the company. Starco is meant to be sending someone round.'

Liz looked at Mrs Grimsby, smiled falsely and then shrugged her shoulders.

'Have you had any news?'

'No.'

'Well, sit down if you want to. We're just glued to the television. No one is telling us anything and Starco is absolutely hopeless. I can't tell you how many times I've called them and they haven't a clue.'

'Do you want something to drink?' Amanda asked, looking at Liz with concern.

'No thanks.'

'Sit down then.'

Liz sat and then Amanda gently placed herself at the other end of the sofa and looked at her, concerned. 'Are you all right?' she asked softly.

Liz nodded her head. 'You?'

Amanda shrugged her shoulders. 'You know.'

The three of them sat saying nothing. Although there was no reason why they should talk, the silence was awkward. Cuthbert was stretched out on the floor enjoying the afternoon sun which was streaming in through the french windows. Every now and again he broke wind and a terrible smell filled the room. At first, everyone pretended to ignore it; after all, it was hardly the moment. But after a while, Liz found it difficult to keep a straight face and when Cuthbert let out a massive fart, she burst into laughter. Within seconds, the two girls were falling around in fits of giggles, spluttering and snorting as they clamped their hands against their mouths to try and stifle the noise.

Mrs Grimsby looked at them as though they were mad. 'What on earth's going on?' she asked, shocked.

Amanda could hardly breathe she was giggling so much. 'It's Cuthbert,' she said. 'He just won't stop.'

'Oh, for goodness' sake. I told you not to give him those fish skins at lunch.'

The two girls burst into another round of laughter. It was such a relief to be able to let all those feelings and emotions out.

'Oh really!' snapped Mrs Grimsby. The girls fell into subdued silence for a moment, yet their eyes were smarting with tears.

'Come on, I'll show you the garden,' said Amanda, pulling herself off the sofa.

Liz had never been shown a garden before. She followed Amanda out on to an immaculately kept lawn.

'Do you like gardening?' Amanda asked, trying to keep a straight face.

'No.'

'Neither do I.' They burst into laughter again, bending over and snorting like donkeys.

'This is Mum's favourite flower bed,' said Amanda looking down. 'Of course it's not looking its best at this time of year.' Amanda looked back through the french windows into the sitting room to see whether her mother was watching them. Then she trampled right across the flower bed, crushing the few remaining flowers and churning the soil up. 'No, it's definitely not looking its best,' she said again. And the two girls staggered off to another part of the garden in fits.

Swung between two elms was a hammock; Amanda leapt up on to it and started to swing backwards and forwards, staring intently at Liz all the time. Eventually she said, 'Liz. I know this isn't really the time, but I want to tell you something.'

'What?' Liz suddenly felt nervous and wondered what was coming.

Amanda bit her lip and looked down at the grass. Then she pulled up her head and said, 'I'm pregnant.'

Liz was shocked. Amanda! Pregnant! It was impossible. Things like that didn't happen to her. They happened to people like Karen . . . or Heather . . . or . . . Not Amanda.

'Surprised?'

'Well . . . yes.'

'Mum doesn't know yet. I don't know how I'm going to tell her.'

Suddenly they heard Mrs Grimsby shouting to them. 'News!' she yelled. 'The news is on.'

The two girls looked at each other, raised their eyebrows and went in.

'News is just coming in that at least twelve men have been picked up from the eighty-eight on board Blue Gorse,' the presenter started. 'Captain Jennings has been involved in the rescue operation and I have him on the line now. What's the situation out there, Captain Jennings?'

A crackly voice came on the line with a still picture of Blue Gorse and the helpline number superimposed on the screen. 'Pretty grim,' said the captain. 'One of the biggest problems is smoke. We just can't get anywhere near the platform itself. We're scanning the sea for survivors and so far have picked up twelve, eight in life rafts and four men have been pulled out of the sea.'

'Surely the evacuation procedure on an installation this size is rigorous. How come you've found only two life rafts?'

'It's difficult to say,' said the captain. 'It's possible that there simply wasn't time to launch them.'

'And for those who've taken the plunge and jumped into the sea?'

'The temperature is fairly mild at the moment so there are survival possibilities. However, the sea itself is on fire, it's covered in burning oil and there are flames everywhere.'

'Captain Jennings, thank you very much.'

Mrs Grimsby sat quite rigid on the sofa. Her face did

not move and she did not shed a single tear. Her feelings were beyond tears. She was convinced her husband was dead. She sensed it, had sensed it right from the very beginning and already an overwhelming feeling of loss and emptiness had engulfed her. She had adored that man. Lived for him. All her life she had looked for a protector, finally found one, and now he had been taken away from her. What was she going to do with her life now? Where would she find anyone else? Would she end up like those career women; living in a flat, working, paying her own mortgage and dealing with insurance companies? The very idea of it made her shudder. She thought she could never live alone although, in many ways, she had always lived alone.

After the news bulletin, Liz decided to leave Mrs Grimsby watching *Humble House*, one of the soaps she had become so addicted to. Amanda followed her to the door. 'Thanks for coming round,' she said, smiling warmly at Liz.

'That's OK.' Liz looked at Amanda. 'What are you going to do?' she asked.

'I don't know. I really don't.' Amanda's chin began to tremble and she fought to keep the tears back. 'You see, my future's no more certain than yours.'

Liz smiled and looked down at her shoes, slightly embarrassed. 'Thanks for telling me.'

Amanda shrugged her shoulders. 'You're the only one who knows.'

'Why me?'

Tears began to seep out of Amanda's eyes. 'I don't know,' she said. 'It just seemed right.'

Liz turned to leave. 'I'll keep in touch. Give you a call tomorrow.'

Amanda smiled through the tears, and then went back into the house.

As Liz rode home from the Grimsbys', she noticed that Boughton was deserted. The whole town was indoors, slurping tea in front of the television. George and Peter Grimsby were not the only men working on Blue Gorse; there was also Teddy Baylis who was a painter and John Foster who was a Catholic and had seven children.

As Liz cycled through the deserted streets, she felt completely burdened and upset by what Amanda had told her. For some reason it had affected her more than the news of the accident. And then, suddenly, she remembered the concert. The concert! The greatest moment of her life was to start in just a few hours and she had forgotten all about it!

In a frenzy of emotion, she slammed on the brakes and screeched to a halt, then she let out a loud wail which came from the very core of her stomach. Suddenly she was hit by every emotion in the book: grief, despair, disappointment, fury. Fury with George. Real fury with him. Again, he had ruined everything for her. Again. How could she play that night when she didn't even know if he was dead or alive. 'Shit!' she shouted and kicked out violently at someone's car. She wanted to smash something. To hit out. To obliterate and destroy.

Suddenly she leapt off her bike, picked it up and, with all her strength, slammed it into the wall of the Crown and Anchor car park.

'Fuuuuck!' she shouted at the top of her voice. 'Fuck you, you bastard!'

When Liz got back to the house, everyone was in pretty much the same position as before. Sheila was still crumpled up on the chair, Nan and Dad still had their hats and coats on and hadn't moved from the sofa, and Arthur was sprawled out on the floor with a can of lager. Only Gary had moved, he was sitting at the kitchen table and Muriel was giving him a lecture when Liz walked in.

'You're the man of the house now,' said Muriel. 'It's up to you to take charge.'

Liz was still furious, but she stopped in her tracks as she crossed the kitchen. 'Why? Is there any news?' she asked nervously.

'Not as such, but you've seen the pictures.'

'Well, you shouldn't jump to conclusions,' Liz shouted storming out of the room and up the stairs.

'Well, excuse me!' said Muriel, putting her hands on her hips in indignation.

'Liz! Where the hell have you been?' Sheila shouted from her chair when she saw her daughter dart through the hall and charge up the stairs. 'Liz!'

'Mind your own bloody business.'

10

George staggered along the smoke-filled corridors of the accommodation module. He called out and looked inside cabins for signs of life, but couldn't see a thing. The bedding and furniture added fuel to the fire and great clouds of black smoke filled the passageways and every available space.

It was a living nightmare. He was barely aware of whether it was real or not. Was he asleep? Was he dreaming? Would he suddenly wake up and find Knockers snoring in the bunk above him or feel the warmth of Sheila's body beside him?

After the first explosion, George had charged out of the dining room shouting to everyone to get to their muster points and follow procedures. But the smoke quickly started to pour down his throat, almost choking him. Coughing and spluttering, he staggered forward, barely able to breathe. He started to feel disorientated and was unsure of where the exit doors were. Yet he knew Blue Gorse better than most, and couldn't just leave men in the accommodation module to perish. After the second explosion, he knew things were getting serious and that he was going to have to give up looking for others and find his own way out.

He started to stagger blindly through the passageways looking for exits. Soon he became caught in a tangle of bodies that was moving in every direction, falling over itself, tentacles crawling along the floor for oxygen. Already the men had started taking off their clothes because of the unbearable heat which was intensifying by the second.

'What the bloody hell happened to the emergency lighting?' someone shouted as he groped his way along the dark corridors.

'Search me.'

'I can't. I can't see a bloody thing.'

'We'll never get out of here alive.'

'Where's the exit?'

'It's got to be straight ahead. Hang on. There's someone here.' George stretched his hand down and fumbled around on the floor, reaching out to touch the soft fleshy body.

'Who is it?'

'Don't know.'

'He's not dead, is he?'

'I don't know.'

George was already feeling weak and breathless himself. Mustering all his strength, he got a grip on the limp body and half carried, half dragged it along the corridor. 'I can't see a thing,' he said. 'Come on. We've got to get out of here, otherwise we'll all be gonners.'

A couple of minutes later someone shouted, 'We've found it. Look the exit's right here.' The men staggered towards the door, eager and praying that soon they would be safely tucked up in a lifeboat. Yet, as they emerged from the accommodation module, their faces fell—the whole rig was on fire. Flames were lashing out from every corner, fireballs were spinning through the air, girders and pipes were crashing down around them and the heat was unbearable.

'Jesus!' one of the men whistled. 'How the hell are we going to get out of this?'

'Let's head for the helideck, maybe a chopper will pick us up.'

'There's no way a chopper can get anywhere near this,' George snapped. He looked down at the body he had hauled out and recognized the thin, sallow features of Jimmy whose face was blackened by smoke and chunks of red hair were singed and burnt. George touched the pulse of the boy's neck, he was still alive but unconscious. George threw him over his shoulder like a sack of potatoes and started to move forward, crouching down to avoid the flames and the smoke.

'Come on,' he shouted. 'We can only go down. The heat's rising and the smoke's coming up through the inside of the jacket. We'll never get to a lifeboat. They're probably all burnt anyway.'

The door to the accommodation module was still open and George could hear choking and coughing inside. He looked back for a moment and caught the eye of a man he had followed out. 'What's your name?' he asked.

'Barry.'

George put out his hand which Barry shook. 'I'm George. Pleased to meet you,' he said. Then he looked back inside the smoke-filled module. 'You know we're going to have to leave them to take their chances.'

'I know,' said Barry. It was almost impossible to see what he looked like his face was so black and the red hard hat he was wearing was melting on to his head. George could see tears glistening in his eyes and watched him sniff loudly and wipe his nose with his sleeve.

Barry looked at Jimmy who was straddled over George's shoulders. 'What about him?'

'He's coming with us.'

Peter Grimsby and the engineer had stayed in the control room as long as they possibly could. Frantically they darted around, flicking switches, pulling levers and issuing empty commands into Tannoys that no one heard except themselves. Grimsby's skin was stretched taut across his ashen white face which glistened with perspiration. 'Why aren't the pumps working?' he shouted maniacally.

'They wouldn't make any difference now,' said the engineer. 'Anyway, the sprinklers are all furred up and probably wouldn't work.'

'Why weren't they replaced?'

'You said it was too expensive.'

Grimsby didn't reply. He continued to flip switches here and there but it was useless; the control room had already been reduced to a mass of wire and rubble, machines were blinking and whirling as they toppled out of the wall and crashed to the ground, and everything was burnt to a black, flaky cinder or melted. Grimsby looked around him in despair, he blamed himself totally for what had happened. 'Nothing's working,' he wailed. 'What are we going to do?'

'Get the hell out of here,' said the engineer. 'Come on, Peter. We've got to get out now.'

As the two men fought their way out of the control room, Grimsby suddenly heard the screaming of a man from one of the cabins nearby. 'I'm going to get him,' he shouted.

'Don't be crazy. You'll never find your way back.'

'I don't care.' Grimsby made his way back past the control room and into the locker room where he had heard the shouting coming from. Coughing and trying to shield his face by pulling his overall across it, he looked around. All he could see was thick black smoke until suddenly, like an apparition, a man with all his clothes on fire came lunging at him, screaming. Grimsby grabbed him and tried to roll him across the floor to extinguish the fire, but a row of lockers came crashing down, trapping both men beneath their boiling hot metal torsos. He struggled and shouted but he knew there was no point. Something inside him didn't want to be rescued. He couldn't leave that rig alive. He didn't deserve to. He could never live with an accident like that on his conscience.

* * *

Jimmy was still flopped over George's shoulder as he and Barry cautiously made their way down the hot metal stairwell to the cellar deck. 'He may be a skinny thing, but he weighs a bloody ton,' George grumbled, trying to ignore the smaller explosions which were constantly going off as the fire spread through the mechanical and electrical workshops. Sparks and fireballs of flaming oil were flying everywhere and the whole rig was disintegrating around them. As he got near the bottom of the ladder, George caught sight of Elvis's body straddled across the roof of the dive control unit where it had been hurled by the first explosion; a thin trickle of blood had already coagulated down the side of his friend's face and clogged up his bushy sideburns. George registered what he saw, but put it to one side of his mind. He couldn't deal with it at that moment. He would mourn his friend later, if he ever managed to get out alive himself.

'Let's try and get over to the north-west corner,' said Barry. 'It doesn't seem to be as badly affected.'

George nodded to a line of storerooms sitting where Barry was pointing. 'Those rooms are full of paint and stripper,' he said. 'If they ignite, they'll go up like a bomb. We've got to go down. Come on, let's go down to the diving platform and try and get off from there.'

But when George and Barry reached the stairwell to the dive platform, the whole thing had collapsed. They could only see a pool of burning diesel below.

Suddenly George caught sight of Paul and Pinocchio; still in their diving gear, they were trying to climb down a rope which they had thrown over the side of the jacket. George called out, 'Is there a way out down there?'

Paul looked up at George vacantly. He saw him but couldn't hear a word he was saying, the roar of the fire was deafening. Paul shrugged his shoulders and carried on down the rope. He was in total shock, terrified. All he wanted to do was to get away from that rig. The fact that he and Pinocchio were still alive was a miracle anyway; as they had clung helplessly to the diving bell, it suddenly started to move and they were literally yanked up at a terrific speed. Colin and another man were winching them up by hand and they eventually landed on the dive platform which was covered with pools of burning oil and drenched in smoke which was infiltrating every hole and crevice on the rig.

'I noticed the umbilicals moving and prayed you were in the bell,' said Colin. 'I won't go into any explanations, I just suggest you get the hell off this death trap.'

'Thanks,' Paul shouted as he pulled off his helmet.

Colin put out his hand and Paul shook it hard. 'Good luck,' he said. 'We all need it.'

All Paul could think of as he and Pinocchio clambered down the thick rope, crashing against the boiling-hot jacket of Blue Gorse, was Belinda. If he got out of this alive, the first thing he was going to do was to marry her. Life suddenly seemed too short to hang around waiting. And what was he waiting for anyway? 'I was thinking of Barbados or Bermuda for the honeymoon,' he shouted at Pinocchio. But Pinocchio couldn't hear him over the din of the flames, or the screams of the men who were literally being incinerated alive, or the crash of huge girders that were falling around them like matchsticks and melting across the decks like butter.

Suddenly a few drops of blood landed on Paul's face. Pinocchio had cut his arm badly by one of the store houses; the cut was deep and blood was pouring out of the wound. Paul looked down at the sea; it was covered with pools of burning oil and looked as though it was on fire. He knew that if they weren't swallowed up by flames first, there were dangerous currents and gas pockets which could easily suck them down. He stopped for a moment, his hands were burning as they slid along the rope and his muscles ached. Above he could see helicopters hovering around them, but he knew they could never get near enough to pick anyone up. Their only hope was the one thing they had always been told not to do: to go into the sea.

George bit his lip and looked around. He had lain Jimmy on the hot metal floor under a fountain of water which was being sprayed on to the rig by rescue vessels which seemed to have materialized out of nowhere. He was tempted just to stay put in the cool water, but knew they had to get down to a lower level and off the rig.

'I've got to bring Jimmy round,' he said to Barry, gently slapping the boy's face and shaking him by the shoulders.

Gradually Jimmy opened his eyes and looked about him. As he registered the scene, a look of terror spread across his face. 'I was changing the beds,' he mumbled.

'Yeah, well, you don't have to worry about that at the moment, Jimmy boy. We're going to have to jump,' said George immediately.

'Jump where?'

'Into the briny, mate. I thought the least we could do was to wake you up before chucking you overboard.'

'But I can't swim.'

'Oh, Jesus. That's all we need.'

Suddenly from the other side of the platform a massive explosion burst into the air and ricocheted across the platform, shaking it from its roots to the top of the flare stack.

'It must be a riser. I knew they'd start to blow,' said George quickly. 'We've got to get off. Now.'

Without waiting a second longer, he and Barry grabbed Jimmy by each arm, lifted him up and ran over to the side of the rig, carrying him between them. 'Hold your nose!' George shouted.

And they jumped 150 feet down into the sea.

The impact of hitting the water almost knocked George out, but then he was revived by the cold water as he sank twenty or thirty feet down. For a while he felt as though he were slipping in and out of consciousness; the cold water brought him round, yet the impact knocked him out again.

Finally he rose to the surface, almost against his will, like a bloated balloon. As he bobbed to the top, he opened his eyes and looked up at the platform; a giant fireball had thundered across it, devouring everything in its path, including scores of men, many of whom had tried to retreat back into the accommodation module for shelter. He knew that it was only a matter of time before the other riser blew; now hundreds of cubic feet of pressurized gas destined for the main processing plant at Boughton were bursting out of the pipe in flames.

As George watched, the fireball continued to rocket into the air like a cannon, spurting flames several hundred feet into the sky. He saw tiny black stick-like men rushing to all sides of the platform and hurling themselves off like lemmings. He watched colleagues and friends he had worked with, spent Christmas with, shared cabins with, eaten with and showered with, leap from the helideck where they had waited in vain to be rescued by chopper. And he saw men crawl along the flare pipe and be roasted alive like pigs on a spit. Around him the sea was on fire, pools of oil and diesel had burst into flames, debris was falling everywhere and he could see that the jacket of the rig itself was beginning to break up and collapse into the sea. He looked around for Barry and Jimmy, but could see no one. Suddenly he began to panic. A wave of terror rushed through his body as he realized the enormity of the disaster. He was no more than a speck in the sea, a blimp of nothingness in a massive uncontrollable inferno. He could be blotted out in a second. He felt out of his depth and totally alone.

'George!'

He looked around and to his great relief saw Barry swimming towards him grinning. 'I don't know what you're looking so bloody happy about,' George shouted. 'She's about to go down.'

'Look behind you.'

George turned and saw a small rescue boat making its

way over to them. Two men were aboard with life jackets, leaning out and signalling for them to hang on.

'What else are we meant to do?' George yelled.

After the rescue boat had picked George and Barry up, it sped around the area they had jumped into looking for other survivors. They quickly found Paul and Pinocchio who had also jumped after the riser had blown, but there was no sign of Jimmy. 'Just do the tour one more time,' said George. 'I'm sure he will have made it. He's a feisty little bloke.'

'We can't,' said one of the rescue men in a broad Norfolk accent. 'It's too dangerous. The whole thing's about to break up. We're putting everyone's lives at risk.'

'Just once more,' said George wiping his charred black face. He had a blanket wrapped around him and sat mournfully at the end of the boat looking down into the water, hoping to see Jimmy's bright face pop up and say, 'Just taking the piss, George.' But it didn't. And as the boat sped back to the main stand-by vessel, George tearfully watched the Blue Gorse gas production platform slowly crumble into the sea like a giant monster that had finally been felled.

Liz sat in the front of Muriel Drain's taxi and stared vacantly out of the window as they rumbled along the flat countryside towards the Town and Country Club. Choosing to play that evening had been the toughest decision she had ever had to make. But she couldn't sit in the house any longer; the morbid sniffling, the arguments and stifling atmosphere were driving her mad. If she hadn't left for the concert, she would have gone somewhere else. Everyone in the house was acting as though George were dead already. They were planning his funeral. Talking about what sort of benefits they would get from Social Security. Would Starco pay them off? If so, they should all go off on a bloody good holiday. Would it be

Spain or the Canaries? What about Italy? Would Nan and Dad go too? There were bound to be reporters. Journalists snooping around. Prying. They were surprised they hadn't turned up on the doorstep already. Apparently they were flooding into Boughton like vultures and the Crown and Anchor and Kings Head were chocka.

Liz felt there was something sick about them all enjoying the drama. She felt quite numb. Didn't feel anything. Didn't think of George. Or of the concert. If anything, she thought about Amanda and felt sorry for her. Perhaps it was a distraction. What did it matter?

Liz turned and looked at Muriel's long protruding nose which presided regally over a large mole from which there sprouted a couple of hairs. Why wouldn't she cut off those hairs? It must be easy enough. A pair of scissors was all that was required. Nothing surgical, surely. Maybe she liked them.

Muriel sensed she was being scrutinized and stared back at Liz. She didn't want any of her lip, she'd had enough to cope with as it was: the day before she had walked into the control room and found her husband, Roger, making a dirty phone call. He said it was the only time he'd ever done it. She knew damn well that some of the wives of men going off-shore had been pestered for months by some pervert. It was blatantly obvious who it was. That day, Muriel went out and bought a mobile phone and had all calls directly routed to it from the taxi office. She wasn't having her husband put her out of business. She had a good mind to report him to the police as it was.

When they reached the Country Club, Liz saw Arabella's mauve hearse sitting in the driveway near the stage entrance. She got out of the car, mumbled her thanks to Muriel, dragged her sax from the back seat and watched the Cortina disappear. Muriel hadn't even wished her luck; she didn't think she should be playing. Thought it was disrespectful. But Liz knew George would want her to play in that concert, whether he was dead or alive. It was what he had always dreamt of.

Liz was amazed to see Sadie helping Arabella set up. The Rhythm Sisters were third on, but they had to get ready and do all the tests to ensure everything was working as it should be.

'Are you all right?' Sadie asked, noticing Liz's subdued air.

'Nervous,' said Liz. She didn't want to talk about the accident. If she brought the subject up, everything else would come with it, and she would never be able to play.

'Excited?'

'Of course.'

'You don't sound it. I'd better get you a drink.'

Sadie disappeared off to the bar while Liz wandered around the stage, wondering what to do with herself and looking out at the vast hall before them. Suddenly she felt terrified. What on earth was she doing there? Her. Liz Dean. What gave her the right to be there? And who said she could play that instrument anyway? 'Oh God!' she muttered under her breath, and went and sat down on a broken chair by the side of the stage.

'Here. This might perk you up.' Sadie handed Liz a beer and stood in front of her, watching her face.

'Thanks for getting me one,' Arabella called out.

'Haven't got enough money.'

Of course, neither Sadie nor Arabella would have known anything about the accident. They never had a clue about anything that happened in the world. Yet Sadie was obviously aware that something was wrong and almost seemed concerned about Liz.

Liz sat back in the chair, ran her hand through her hair and smiled weakly. 'I'm OK,' she said. 'Something came up, that's all. I'll tell you later.'

'Are you sure?'

Liz nodded and took a large slurp from her glass. 'Better get the bugle out of the box and warm up a bit,' she said brightly.

* * *

George and Barry sat on a pile of ropes on the deck of one of the stand-by vessels; a musty old blanket was wrapped around each of them and they cupped a mug of tea in their hands. Mesmerized by the spectacle before him, George watched as the flames continued to soar relentlessly into the sky, giving off dense clouds of black smoke which trailed across the horizon, turning the day into night. He felt as though he were in hell.

Barry had been silently weeping since they had been hauled on to the stand-by vessel and taken down to the damp hold where they were given ill-fitting yet dry overalls to put on. They were given a cup of tea, a blanket and, when there seemed no obvious injuries for the over-burdened medic to sort out, they were allowed to wander back to the deck. Barry couldn't stop himself weeping, it just poured out of him and, after a while, he didn't even bother trying to hide it. It was a release. A safety valve that relieved just a little of the shock, the struggle, the horror, the pain. He couldn't cope with it. No one could. It was just too much.

And yet George felt numb. He felt as though he were a spectator watching a film. As though none of it was real. The men who were being hauled ashore screaming, their faces bright red and skinned, their hair burnt off, some half naked, seemed like illusions. He was living in a nightmare. Looking at that inferno, he wondered how any of them had survived. How had he survived? Why had he survived? Why him and not that dead bloke they were trying to haul on to the stand-by vessel?

Tea in hand, George sat watching a huddle of men wrestling with bodies the rescue boats were bringing in.

'OK, take it easy now,' one shouted as they tried to get the corpse aboard the stand-by vessel with as much dignity as possible. As George watched them struggle with the dead and the wounded, he suddenly wondered what the hell he was doing just sitting there drinking tea. He put down his cup, leapt up and rushed over to the side of the boat to help.

'This one's had it,' one of the men shouted from the rescue boat.

'OK. We've got a grip,' George yelled as he leaned over and grabbed the man underneath his armpits; someone else lifted the feet and, between them, they hauled the body up and over the side of the boat as though it were a lump of meat. Then, as gently as possible, they lowered him down and laid him on the deck floor. George stood back and looked at the dead man; the thick black smoke had plunged the day into night before its time, but George could still make out his face, it was Colin Miller from dive control.

Everyone in the band was getting nervous. People were beginning to arrive and mill around the hall with drinks in hand, greeting long-lost friends and chatting in subdued voices. By now the girls had been herded into a poky dressing room which was normally a ladies loo for the staff. Other artists and management kept popping in: 'Oops, wrong room, sorry.' Liz let Arabella and Sadie worry about the concert. She felt strangely calm about it. It didn't seem to matter any more. Nothing did really. As Sadie and Arabella fussed over their make-up, Liz slipped out and wandered along the corridor to a public telephone. She picked up the receiver and dialled home. Sheila answered almost immediately, 'Hello,' she said, sounding mad. 'Hello. Hello.'

'It's me, Mum.'

'Oh. Well, don't stay on too long. You're jamming the line.'

'I only called to see if there'd been any news.'

'Of course there hasn't. I'd tell you if there had.'

'Yes, but . . . ' Liz swallowed, took a deep breath and

stopped herself. This wasn't the time to stir Sheila up. 'OK, Mum. I just wanted to know. I'll get off the line now.'

And the telephone went dead. Sheila had hung up without another word. No 'good luck', no 'goodbye'. Nothing.

Liz took another deep breath, swallowed again and replaced the receiver.

When Liz got back to the dressing room, Sadie was applying one layer of make-up after another.

'How's anyone going to know who you are,' Arabella grunted.

Sadie ignored her and carried on in what she thought was the spirit of the true professional.

Suddenly there was a knock on the door and the club manager came in. He was a short, round man with a bald head and wearing a tweed three-piece suit. 'Everything ready, girls?' he asked grinning, showing an uneven row of tobacco-stained teeth.

The *girls* virtually ignored him.

'Good.' He rubbed his hands together gleefully. 'Not so many as we hoped for, I'm afraid. They're all out watching that disaster.'

'What disaster?' Sadie snapped as she laced up her black boots.

'I can see you've got your finger on the pulse. The gas rig that blew up this afternoon. Just off the coast. Hundreds killed they say. They're bringing them all in now. Dead and alive. I'm afraid we can't compete with something like that.'

Suddenly Sadie looked across at Liz who was leaning against the wall, biting her lip and looking down at the floor. 'Liz,' she said, 'your father works on the rigs, doesn't he?'

Liz could contain herself no longer. She fled from the room, rushed along the corridor and on to the carefully manicured club lawns. She threw herself behind a hedge and crouching down began to sob. And sob and sob and sob. Heaving all the grief, all the sadness and despair and fury out of her system.

The stand-by vessel which George had been taken to finally left the waters surrounding Blue Gorse and chugged as fast as it could to another platform several miles away. The men clambered aboard; some had to grapple with a ladder while the badly wounded were winched up in a basket. As he hauled himself up, George felt watched by hundreds of pairs of horrified eyes. These belonged to the men who had seen the whole thing and, even though Blue Gorse was ten miles away, had been shocked to their shoes by the sight of the inferno raging on the horizon.

Suddenly George heard a squawk. He looked up and saw Elvis's bright blue parrot perched on one of the jacket girders, watching the men climb aboard. George grinned to himself. 'You sly bastard,' he said and reached across to the bird which seemed to understand perfectly and jumped on to his arm, grateful to be rescued for a second time.

Twenty minutes later, a helicopter transported twenty men, four badly wounded, and one blue parrot back to Boughton. Like school children, they allowed themselves to be ferried along and when they arrived, various officials from Starco were there to greet them and fend off the press. The badly wounded were immediately rushed to ambulances which roared off into the night, their lights flashing and sirens blaring. And those men who could walk wandered around a small reception room shivering and dazed, feeling vulnerable and weak.

At one point an officious-looking man in a well-cut, expensive suit stood in the middle of the room and cleared his throat. 'OK. Now, I know you've had a rough time of it, but before you go home everyone's got to go to hospital for a check up,' he said in an American accent. 'There are ambulances outside to take you. But before you go, please give us your details so we can contact your families.'

George wandered up to the official and put up his hand cautiously. 'Um, excuse me.'

'Yes.'

'I've lost a shoe. Look. One of the blokes from the stand-by vessel gave it to me and . . . well . . . it's gone.'

'Don't worry about that. We'll sort out some shoes for you. Do you need any money?' The official took a large wad of bank notes out of his pocket, peeled a few off, and stuffed them into George's palm.

'Thank you very much.' George pocketed the money and wandered over to Barry. 'I'd get over there if I were you. He's just given me two hundred quid.'

'Dirty money,' said Barry contemptuously.

'Money all the same.'

But Barry didn't look very interested, he was staring ahead of him vacantly, his eyes still filled with tears.

George looked around the room and then nodded down at the parrot he was cradling inside an old jacket he had been given to wear.

'Me and Fred are pushing off,' he said.

'You can't. We've all got to go to hospital.'

'Oh, bollocks. There's nothing wrong with me. Look. Not a mark. And he's all right.'

'Yes, but there might be something else.'

George waved Barry away. 'Nothing a good night's sleep won't sort out,' he said. He slapped Barry on the back and wandered away, through the Arrivals Hall and out into the sharp night air. A fresh breeze was blowing and George stood there for a while, breathing, just enjoying the sensation of standing on firm ground, even though he only had one shoe on and the gravel was digging into his foot.

'The ambulances are over there on the right,' he heard a voice shout out to him.

'Righto.' He waved back and, stroking the parrot's silky

head, turned in the opposite direction and walked towards a line of taxis.

'Oh, my God, Cas has turned up,' Arabella groaned as she peered from behind the curtain, nervously watching the hall fill up. 'Typical. I haven't seen him all week, and now he decides to ruin things here.'

'You worry. My mum's down there,' said Sadie who was now fully made up and looked a bit like a Geisha girl in drag. 'I told her not to come. Now I really feel nervous.'

Liz didn't say anything. She had managed to splash her face with water and then applied loads of moisturizer to it.

The act before them was Linda Belinda, a girl double-act in which a pair of twins belted out 'It's in his Kiss' and 'Dancing Queen'. As they were taking their bows to unenthusiastic, polite applause, the Rhythm Sisters stood in the wings, waiting. For once they were all quiet; Arabella was tapping her foot on the floor to a song she was playing in her head, Sadie was biting her nails and looked like a wild woman possessed, and Liz felt sad and lonely because the other two at least had someone there, even if it was only Cas and Sadie's mum.

'How many do you reckon were killed, then?' the taxi driver asked George. He couldn't believe he actually had someone in his cab who'd been on that rig. It was the biggest drama to hit Boughton, ever. The place was swarming with journalists and TV crews. The pubs were doing a roaring trade, shops were staying open late, and he had doubled his fares.

George shrugged his shoulders, irritated by the question. 'I don't bloody know, do I?' he said.

'Sorry, mate,' said the driver. 'Hope you don't mind me asking. It's just that, well, we've been following it all. So to meet someone who's seen it all first hand . . . well, you know.'

George was quiet for a moment. 'What do you mean following it?' he asked quietly.

'You can't get away from it. It's on the telly, the radio. Everyone's talking about it. There's journalists and TV people everywhere.'

George was quiet again. Suddenly he thought of everyone at home; of Sheila, of Nan and Dad, the kids. Did they know about the accident? It had never occurred to him that life on the rigs could connect with life on shore at all. For him they were two totally separate worlds. He expected to just walk into the house, surprise everyone by his early arrival, and that would be that. He'd probably go down the pub. He hadn't thought that they might know about this accident and be worrying about him.

Sitting there, as the taxi waited to pass through TV crews and large lorries blocking the roads, George thought of Jimmy and his puny little body floating around somewhere out there in the sea, waterlogged, tangled up with all that metal and garbage; a minnow in a sea of sharks. Then his thoughts turned to Gary, his son, and the rest of the family. He wondered if they would be glad to see him. Perhaps they had secretly hoped to have got him off their hands. Would their faces fall when he walked in and they realized he was still alive? He didn't deserve to be. They all hated him, he knew. His eyes filled with tears as he sat there and acknowledged this fact, perhaps for the first time ever. George knew this was a turning point in his life. He knew things would never be the same again.

As the taxi crawled slowly through the flashing cameras and rumbled across the spaghetti of television wires covering the coast road, they suddenly passed a sign to The Town and Country Club. 'Hang on a minute,' George shouted to the cab driver. 'What day is it today?'

The Rhythm Sisters had ploughed through their first number, 'Call Me', without any major hitches, even though Sadie was having trouble reaching the note for the last 'me' of each verse. Liz was doing little more than go through the motions; she felt she was in a dream and that the audience was separated from her by a thick glass screen. The lights were blinding and giving her a headache. And she knew that if she looked at the swarm of people below just once, she'd lose her nerve completely. The next number was her solo—'Stormy Weather'. The big one. Her big chance.

As Sadie and Arabella crashed out the last few notes of 'Private Dancer', Liz took the sax from her mouth and bent down to pick up the glass on the floor. She took a long slow sip of water and tried to ignore her trembling hands. The room was filled with smoke, all she could see was the lights, all she could feel was the surge of bodies and the heat. She took another sip and, as she bent down to put the glass back on the floor, she saw, from the corner of her eye, George's burnt black face looking up at her, his eyes white and shining proudly, a beaming smile stretching from cheek to cheek.

She could barely believe her eyes. There he was. Right there, just a few feet away. Watching patiently and smiling. She looked again. Was that a parrot he had in his pocket? He put his thumbs up, grinned, pointed to the parrot and nodded. He was there. Her father was there, for her, and he had a parrot in his pocket. Typical. Everything would be all right now. She smiled, put the sax to her mouth and started to play.